D0249997

MYSTICAL ROSE

MYSTICAL ROSE

RICHARD SCRIMGER

Doubleday Canada

Copyright © Richard Scrimger 2000
Paperback edition 2001

All rights reserved. The use of any part of this publication reproduced, transmitted, in any form or by any means, electronic, mechanical, photocopying, recording, or otherwise, or stored in a retrieval system, without the prior consent of the publisher — or, in the case of photocopying or other reprographic copying, a licence from the Canadian Reprography Collective — is an infringement of the copyright law.

Doubleday Canada and colophon are trademarks.

Canadian Cataloguing in Publication Data
Scrimger, Richard, 1957–
        Mystical Rose
ISBN 0-385-25954-9 (bound)   ISBN 0-385-25955-7 (pbk.)
I. Title.
PS8587.C745M97 2000   C813'.54   C00-930183-6
PR9199.3.S37M97 2000

Cover photograph: Cheryl Koralik/Photonica
Cover design by Greg Stevenson
Printed and bound in Canada

Published in Canada by
Doubleday Canada, a division of
Random House of Canada Limited

Visit Random House of Canada Limited's website:
www.randomhouse.ca

TRANS 10 9 8 7 6 5 4 3 2 1

To You, with thanks for all Your help

Cause of our joy, pray for us.
Spiritual vessel, pray for us.
Vessel of honour, pray for us.
Vessel of singular devotion, pray for us.
Mystical rose, pray for us.
Tower of David, pray for us.
Tower of ivory, pray for us.
House of gold, pray for us.

From the Litany of the Blessed Virgin

1

Finding

Your eyes are very dark. And sad. They're so sad. Why is that? What have You done that's so terrible? You're okay — what am I saying, of course You're okay. You don't have anything to be sad about. Cheer up. Dry those tears. Turn that frown upside down. You can do it. You can do anything.

So why are You crying? There, now You've got me doing it too.

Water. Tears are water. All around me is water, rising, slopping against everything. Rising inside of my lungs, choking me. Just like it was the last time. Oh, Mama. All that commotion, and I can't breathe. Cold, so cold.

A long time ago now.

How much has happened, how many births and deaths and givings in marriage, heartaches and headaches, love and laughter, wars and breakfasts. How much life.

Harriet's always telling everyone how much I love life. My daughter, don't blame me for the name; it was Robbie's choice. He laughed when I suggested Gert, my best friend in grade school. No, I'm serious, I said, and he laughed some more. Mother loves life, says Harriet. A wonderful woman, my daughter. I hope I had as much energy when I was her age.

Here she is now, standing beside You. Does she see You? Her mouth is open but she's not talking to You. She reaches towards me, huge white hands — she got them from Robbie too, along with the name. My hands are fine and delicate, pretty hands, my mother used to say. How could anyone mistake you for a boy, with such pretty hands, my baby? Pretty hands grabbing her veil, her big hat, her cambric handkerchief. Oh dear, I'm drowning again.

Harriet wipes my face. It feels nice. She says, There there, but I don't know where she means. This is a hospital, there's only here here.

Her hands are as cold as grade school. I used to get there before the teacher, who came in a cart all the way from Cobourg, six miles each way, almost two hours in the winter. I had to walk a mile down the Harwood Road to Precious Corners, and by the time I got to the schoolhouse I'd be frozen. A beautiful time of day, the sun rising over snow-covered fields. But cold. First one to school had to light the stove. The kindling used to smell of mice and dust. The fire was friendly and warm. Sometimes the boys used to throw each other's homework in.

Four years old and no daddy. He's off at The War, my mama told me. So was my friend Gert's daddy. He was a farmer too, like my daddy. Mama cried. So did Gert's mama. She had red hair and a face like a harvest moon. What's The War? I asked, but Mama wouldn't answer. What's The War? I asked the teacher. A terrible thing.

I stayed away from the school in the spring, to help Mama and Victor with the farm. Lettuces and cabbages and corn to plant and pigs to feed, until the pigs all got sick. Six years old and no school.

The teacher would come by in the evenings, to tell me what I'd missed. She brought the newspaper with her. There's been a terrible battle at a place called Loos, she'd say. Or Gallipoli. All the places were strange sounding. Mama cried. The newspaper smelled like the inside of the teacher's coat pocket. Then the letter arrived from Ottawa, saying Daddy was coming home. He got sick just like the pigs, but they died and he didn't. Mama and I met him at the station in town, with all the neighbours. He hugged us and then limped over to talk to Gert's mama. She fainted.

The leg wound got better, but Daddy was different inside. He didn't care about anything any more, as if The War had taken out the part of him that minded. The seed corn came up too late, and the cabbages got holes in them, and he didn't mind. Something broke into the barnyard in the middle of the night, maybe a coyote, and took our chickens, and he didn't mind. My teacher died of the flu, and they closed the school until they could find someone else, and he didn't mind. For days and days he wouldn't get out of bed. Mama did her best with the harvest, and neighbours gave us help and meat, but the snow lasted a long time that year, and some days we had nothing to eat but cabbages and stale bread. We needed new furniture, Mama said so, and I needed new clothes, but Daddy said he didn't mind the table and chairs we had. And Rose looks fine, he said. He sat by himself at the dinner table, close to the bottle of poison. That's what Mama called it. His hair was grey.

I would have been ten when Victor broke his leg and couldn't get up. I saw him first and ran to the house for help. Daddy came with me to the barn, stood outside the stall while Victor flopped around in his stall. I was crying. Daddy watched for a long time, then went to the house for his gun. I stayed in my room, and

Daddy fired four shots at Victor's head. I heard them. Horses have hard heads, you have to hit them just right. Victor would have told me that, later. Or do I mean Uncle Brian?

Is Dr. Berman in Your way? He's new. He has an odd first name — Sunday, would it be — and he introduces himself by it. You could ask him to move, You know. Or You could blast him with the power of the worm that dieth not. I wonder what he's saying to my daughter. His teeth are very expressive.

Harriet is my daughter, Harriet Rolyoke. Not Zimmerman, as it could have been — poor Geoff, I can still see him on his knee in our front room, with his manicure and the tufts of hair poking out of his nose when he smiled. Not Bluestone, though she did seem to like him, and he had every reason to be grateful to her. Harriet Rolyoke. The name she was born with. I tried and tried, but there's no pleasing some people. You can't afford to pick and choose, I told her, not meaning to make her feel bad, but facts are facts and no boys fought over her the way they used to fight over me. Every day I see plain women with husbands, I told her. D'you want to end up all alone? She'd laugh and pat my arm. Even when she was young, she always seemed to be laughing at me. I may have a better sense of humour than I know.

Uncle Brian was the family black sheep and Daddy's big brother. His commercial success in Belleville and then Toronto, and the opportunities he talked about in the letters home to Gloucestershire, convinced my daddy to come to Ontario with his bride. Uncle Brian bought two second-class passages as a wedding present, and drove all the way to New York to meet us. He was a banker; all I'd have seen of him when we arrived was his lavender spats. The sound of his motor car — the first I'd ever heard — buzzed in my ears like the dying summer. I listened for it each time he came to Precious Corners to visit. I loved to ride in it, feeling the wind on my face, watching the world spin past faster than thought.

He visited less often after the bank took away his car and his salary and moved him to northern Ontario, but he was with us at the Port Hope station when Daddy came home from The War. The spats were grey by this time, and stained. Like Uncle Brian's success, I guess. By then I could see above his knees, to the lean hams and bony brisket beneath the threadbare woollen suit that no longer had a pocket watch to complete it, nor a diamond stickpin, nor a dangling white scarf, cashmere coat, or stiff Homburg hat. The War had been hard on him too. Welcome back, he said to Daddy, shaking hands on the doorstep. His hands were bigger than Daddy's, and his nose was longer. He wouldn't stay to dinner.

I'm dying, aren't I. That's why You're here. That's why You look so sad — I guess mine isn't a beautiful death. That's what Mrs. McAllister used to say, Didn't so-and-so make a beautiful death. A sour long-faced lady, her husband George owned the mill in Harwood. She wore hats with flowers — carnations and purple larkspur, I think, unless I'm getting confused with what the flowers mean: *pride* and *haughtiness*. She used to ask Mama and me into her parlour for tea and little cakes while our corn was being ground. She didn't invite everyone, but Mama was English English, and that mattered in Ontario in the twenties. I don't know what I would have been. A polite little girl, I guess, and as clean as lye soap and scrubbing could make me, for all I was dressed poor. Was Mrs. McAllister's father really a concert pianist? She'd tell us that, pointing to the piano as a kind of proof, but I never heard it from anyone else. I asked Mama once and she said she wasn't sure, meaning she doubted it. You know the truth, of course. Maybe I will too, soon. A vicious lady, Mrs. McAllister, but kind enough to me. I wonder, was her death beautiful? I can't see it, somehow.

Uncle Brian had arranged a mortgage on the farm when he worked at the bank. Mama wrote to him for help the spring after Victor died and we couldn't put any crop in the field, but the letter came back inside another envelope. It was a surprise to see his gaunt, spare figure in the kitchen a few months later, to hear his voice, so like Daddy's, ask Mama if we could put him up for a while since he was out of a job, and maybe he could help out around the farm for a bit. Hello, Rose, he said to me, twisting his knuckles together. Mama didn't say anything.

Have a drink, said Daddy, pushing the bottle forward.

And so Uncle Brian came to live with us. A broken man, life trickling out of him like sawdust. Daddy didn't mind. He was a burnt-out shell himself, with gypsies camping inside his mind. My mother and I toiled with our heads down, fearful of what today would bring.

Lady Margaret Rolyoke was a thin dry woman, beautiful from a distance. A white orchid of a woman: exotic, colourless, odorless. The sort of woman men don't need. She was Lady Margaret because she was the daughter of a duke. Her husband was plain Mr. Rolyoke, Philadelphia Pennsylvania in the winter, Cobourg Ontario in the summer. You know, I still think about them. All the chances missed. Needless pain, prolonged until it ceases to matter, like a stone in your shoe that you get used to walking with, until you take it out and then you think, How could I have gone on like that? He's been dead for almost fifty years, and she for ten or more, and I'm still limping.

I knew the Rolyoke place before I went there to work. Everyone in Cobourg and Hamilton township knew the huge log palace, one of dozens of stately homes just a ferry ride away from Rochester, New York. The best air in North America, pure ozone, they said, optimal climatic conditions — I wonder if they really were. Cottesmore Hall, Hamilton House, Strathmore, Bagnall Hall, Heathcote, Sidbrook. Oh my. The names bring back a hint of vanished glory, like a whiff of old perfume clinging to a fur coat at the back of a closet. And all the grand homes needed seasonal attention from local plumbers and glaziers, butchers and fruiterers, gardeners and house servants.

I met Lady Margaret by accident. Mama would have spoken to her about me, but I'd never seen her. Early in the morning on my first day and I was trying to find the servants' entrance so I asked the first person I saw. Herself as it happened, taking a walk in the garden. I'm lost, I said, and she took me by the elbow — a curious gesture, more like a police officer than a friend — and led me around the far side to the very door. You must be the flower girl, she said. I was still in mourning for Daddy. When she saw the band she expressed very civil condolences. I hope you'll be happy here, she said. I ducked my head and she walked me into the back kitchen and told that bitch Parker to call Adam, and meanwhile to be especially nice to me. I was sixteen. Parker smiled and said, Certainly my lady, and the minute we were alone she slapped me spinning against the far wall.

Black boots with buttons, cotton stockings, and two petticoats, even in the middle of the hottest summer in years, long loose housedress the colour of pale coffee, with a white apron and cap. Everything from the skin out starched until it stood by itself, and God forbid — well, You know what I mean — that you should have to scratch. No wonder Parky was always in a bad temper, she sweated so. The uniform was the Duchess of Ainslie's design, Robbie told me later. Lady Margaret's mother. I would have met her at the wedding if she'd been there.

My first garden party. Admiral Byrd had just flown over the North Pole and everyone was talking about it. Only he wasn't an admiral yet, was he? When they weren't talking about him they were talking about the Sesquicentennial Exposition; my, I got sick of that. The Pennsylvania Museum and School of Industrial Art, I can hear Parky's voice now. Such elegance, she said. You wouldn't have understood it, Rose.

The south lawn, also known as the lake lawn because it went right down to the pebbled shore of Lake Ontario, on a late afternoon in

June. The sun burned a hole in the middle of an empty blue sky, the shadows were thick under the maples, and the wavetops glistened and sparkled. There was just enough of a breeze to ruffle skirts and keep away the flies. I was in charge of the muffins. Really, muffins. I was to go around with the covered tray, making sure that the ladies had an opportunity to partake. Would you care for a muffin, madam? This was my line — I only had to rehearse it a couple of times to get it right. Parker didn't think I was refined enough. Mr. Rolyoke's wrong about you, she said. You're not ready for company. You've only been here a week. You're an outdoor girl, she told me, withering. A gardener's help. Can't even hold a tray steady, can you?

Try to walk across the kitchen, Miss Rose, suggested Mr. Davey gently. He was the one who drove the cars — kindling, that's not the word. Why can't I think of the word? A fat man, not too old, with a kind word for everyone, he'd been badly burnt in The War. We were all a little afraid of his appearance. He and Parker were the only servants who went south with the Rolyokes in September. I walked across the kitchen towards him, offering the tray and saying my line, only I hesitated when I was about to call him madam. I felt myself blushing and he smiled — that is, his mouth twisted sideways. Looked hideous, but I knew it was a smile. Walking back across the kitchen I tripped over Parker's outstuck foot, made quite a din. She sniffed when Mr. Davey helped me up. Thanks, I told him. He shook his head. Not at all, Miss Rose, you don't weigh more than a feather.

The ladies at the party were nice to me too. So young, they said, which I didn't feel. So tiny, they said, which I wasn't, not really, just undernourished. So pretty — well, I suppose I *was* pretty. I'm sorry, Harriet, but I was, with my dark hair (though it wouldn't curl no matter how hard I tried), dark eyes, straight teeth that gave me no pain, eyebrows that curved naturally. Ah, but it's a long time since I looked like that. The boys at school thought me a beauty. I remember very well the day one of them brought the family cart to take me home. The harness was decked out in ribbons, and the old Clydesdale's coat and mane were combed until they shone like gold. The looks the other boys gave — now what was the Clydesdale boy's name?

My uncle suggested the hunting trip. He and Daddy were sitting at the kitchen table with a bottle of wine they'd made in an old swill tub out of cabbage hearts and sugar, and Mama and I were arguing about whether I could go to the Park Theatre with Gert to see *The Big Parade*. David — I mean John Gilbert — was in it. Mama was saying it was too expensive and I was saying, Oh please. Uncle Brian finished his glass and banged it down on the table.

Moose, he said. The only animal worth shooting. He blinked. The end of his nose twitched. He didn't look like a hunter.

Daddy stared at him. Said nothing.

I've shot many a moose, said Uncle Brian. The woods around Kirkland Lake are full of them. You want to aim just behind the foreleg, he said, sighting along his outstretched hands as if, trembling from the wine, they cradled a gun.

The single oil lamp, hung on a nail from a low beam, flickered and died, leaving the kitchen in smoky firelight. Romantic but chilly. I could feel the wind blowing through an assortment of cracks in the walls and windows.

I was sick of the place, sick of the constant tension of uncertainty, not knowing how much there'd be to eat or what quiet horror Daddy and Uncle Brian would get up to — one night one of them found a rabbit cowering under a corner of the outhouse and brought it to the cleared table. They wouldn't let it go and they wouldn't kill it, but let it hop uncertainly up and down the bare wood, laughing every time it relieved itself. After an hour the thing just lay down, it was so tired, and Uncle Brian bashed it with a brick.

Why can't I go to the movies? I said loudly to Mama. Gert's going. Everyone else is going. Why can't I do anything except sit here in the dark? It's not right, I said. Fifteen years old and telling my Mama right and wrong. But I knew, and so did she.

I'd like to let you go, Rosie, but we need the money.

But it's my money, I said.

You want a big-game rifle, said Uncle Brian, pouring wine. That popgun of yours won't do the trick. A moose'd just laugh at your old buckshot loads. Now John Habemayer over the other side of Burnham Road, he's got a proper rifle. Used to hunt a lot — you've seen the heads on his wall, haven't you? I wonder if he'd let us borrow it for a few days. There's moose in the Ganaraska Woods.

Daddy didn't say anything.

It's my money in the sugar can, I said.

Mama frowned. It won't cost but a quarter, I said. There's still more than a dollar left over from my flowers.

I remember weeding, hunched over a row of newly planted greens, digging and pulling until my back ached. Every year the same, as far back as I could remember. As soon as I was old enough to stand, I was old enough to pull weeds. Hawkweed and chickweed mostly: *quicksighted* and *assignation*. And nettle: *slander*. I thought of them as tough stinkers and evil creepers.

And then, shuffling forward like an old woman, my back bent, I came upon an unexpected — You know the flower I mean, the white wildflower, what's it called, Angelica, no, dammit, I mean undammit. Why can't I remember the name? Anyway, there it was in the middle of a row of peas, and I couldn't bear to pull it up by the roots. So beautiful, with its white petal wings and golden face, smiling up at me, and there were a couple more nearby, crowding the shoots in the next row. I came back that evening, and carried the flowers to a bed I had dug along the border of the east field, far out of the way. The soil was thin, mostly gravel. I cleared a space for the daisies — I don't know why I couldn't think of the name before — and transplanted them. All that summer I collected wildflowers from among the wormeaten vegetables, and replanted them in my little garden.

I wonder if after all that was the main attraction of it — it was mine. I'd have been twelve or thirteen, and there wasn't much I could call my own. The miracle a few years back was a warm memory, flowers appearing like magic on our front steps, but they weren't my flowers. Poor Mama had had half a mind to dig them up and take them back to Mr. Cuyler.

But this was charity from the land itself, from You, I suppose, and Mama actually smiled when she saw the garden. Doesn't that look nice, she said. She made a point of collecting samples for me, and by the end of the summer my flowers made a border all down the eastern fence — almost half a mile. I had enough of a patch to be noticed by the neighbours on that side of us, the ones related to the McAllisters.

Mrs. McAllister mentioned to me and Mama in the summer, when our corn was being ground and we were in the parlour drinking tea and Daddy and Uncle Brian were up at the mill drinking whisky, that cut flowers were fetching a penny a bunch in town.

Cut flowers. What if they don't come back? I asked Mama. What if they die and don't come back? She hugged me. They will, she said. So I dragged myself out to the east field in the morning, and stood at the edge of the garden as the wind came up and bowed the white heads, and the purple, and the pink and yellow. And I took the old scythe with a new cutting edge I'd put on it, and went to work killing my garden.

I made nine dollars that first year, selling bunches of flowers from the back of Gert's daddy's cart. Her mama would have remarried by then, and Gert's new daddy had a livery business in town, which, and he was a very generous man, is how come we could get our corn to the mill without Victor. Gert still sat next to me in school, and liked me even if the boys mostly ignored her. She did, didn't she? I'd hate to be wrong about that. I liked her too. Nine dollars was two weeks' wages at the furniture factory or tannery. I gave the money to Mama and went out to my garden and cried, because it was just part of the east field now, bare and brown, and winter was coming.

Please let me go to the movies, I said to my mama, the year my daddy died.

A full-grown moose can derail a train, said Uncle Brian. I remember being on a sleeper from Sudbury to someplace and all of a sudden in the middle of the night — Bam! — like the end of the world. Throws me right out of the bunk. I'm thinking we're caught in a landslide, and then I see the porter shaking his fists out the window. Fucking moose, he says, means we're stuck here until they can send another engine. Timiskaming, that's where we were going. Only we're not. And then a huge shape lumbers past the window. I see it against the snow — a moose. It's walking, and the train is derailed.

Daddy poured a drink for each of them.

Don't go to the movies, whispered Mama. Don't leave me here alone, Rose.

Robbie wasn't there the first summer I worked for the Rolyokes, the summer when Admiral Byrd flew over the Pole, and Gert's mom went crazy because Rudolph Valentino was found dead, and Houdini — the scariest thing I heard that summer — Houdini stayed underwater in a coffin for an hour and a half. I almost fainted when Mr. Davey read me the story from the newspaper. Robbie was off in Europe learning French, or shooting, or sailing.

I didn't even know there was a young Rolyoke. No one spoke of him. It wasn't until we were sitting alone with the world beneath us that I realized who he was.

I say, there! he called to me, a nicely dressed young man, squinting up. What are you doing? It's too early for chestnuts, and besides, this is a private —

His voice broke off. He stared harder. I should say we were about forty feet apart, vertically. I was halfway up a big chestnut tree with a coil of rope over my shoulder.

You're a girl, he declared in surprise. I suppose it was the workman's trousers that hung on my skinny hips. They'd had to find a pair from the boy who polished boots and silver. Not that a lot of girls wear dresses to climb trees. Did I blush? I didn't like to be mistaken for a boy.

He wasn't local, I could tell by his accent, and because I didn't know him. I took him for a guest at the big log house. I edged out along my branch, keeping a good handhold, and reached up to tie one end of the rope to the middle of the rotten bough above me. The air around me was heavy with dust and mould. A squirrel, scolding from a nearby tree, sounded very loud. I wiped cobweb out of my eyes.

Careful, he said. Oh, be careful.

Now it would have been my turn to be surprised. Concern was not something I was used to hearing in the voices of guests. Not concern for me. Guests belonged to a different world. Rich, seasonal transient, foreign, they looked and talked and acted in a way that would have been impossible for me and my friends. Horse shows and polo matches and car rallies through the town. My friends would line King Street East to stare at the fashions and jewels on their way to the Arlington Hotel for the Saturday Grand Hop. Imagine a party with guests filling the whole lawn, and electric lights strung out along the hedges, and a dance band playing in the middle of the swimming pool filled with orchids! Mr. Davey told me about it; he'd driven the Rolyokes. A swimming pool filled with flowers and music — I still think it's a beautiful idea.

Oh, be careful! He watched closely, never moving from where he stood but never quite still. His hands fluttered about on their own. He jigged up and down, as if he had springs inside his clothes, while I looped the rope over a sturdy upper bough and threw the coil down to Adam, the head gardener.

Excuse me, Mr. Robbie, he said.

Oh, hello, Adam, said the young man.

Ready, Rose? called Adam. I turned around carefully on my branch, reaching into the crotch of the tree where I'd left the saw.

Rose? said the young man. Rose?

Straddling my branch, I took a quick look down through the criss-cross of leaves before starting to saw.

Rose? he said to Adam.

Better stay out of the way, Mr. Robbie. That branch is going to come down.

And that's how you met? Wow! Talk about romance! Ruby exclaimed. You a servant girl and he a son of the manse. You had it all, Rosie, she said. Her face was flushed. Of course she'd had a bit to drink by then.

Wait, there's more, I said. It gets better.

I must have had a bit too. And yet it wouldn't have been too late in the day, would it? We were upstairs, above Ruby's hat shop. I could see the lake through her front window, which looked down Glen Manor Road. Late summer afternoon, Sunday, and quiet. You wouldn't believe how quiet Toronto could be on summer Sundays in the forties. I wonder where Harriet was. Movies? Band practice?

What's a manse? I asked.

Nothing like that ever happens to me, said Ruby. Her hair hung down like a curtain in front of her face.

What about Montgomery? I said. I'd have met him by then.

What about him? He's a good-for-nothing, a salesman. A great guy to have around if you want to buy a knife, but not romantic.

Yes he is, I said. He can be. Anybody can be romantic. Romance is about you, not about circumstances, I said.

She tried to digest this, but it wouldn't go down. Bullshit, she said. And upended her glass. Rum, I think. That went down. She usually drank rum. Her father had been in the merchant marine.

I sawed through the big rotten bough, but it didn't move. Adam shouted at me to hurry up. I pushed and pulled, but I couldn't free the rotten branch from the surrounding network of leaves and interlocking smaller branches. I cursed the stickiness and the bugs, cursed the loyalty of little fingers clutching the healthy parent tree which was no longer attached to it. Finally I climbed up, wedged myself against the rippled trunk and kicked at the fresh-cut end of the rotten branch, a gleaming white oval. It wouldn't budge.

The branch is stuck! I called down to Adam.

I felt a vibration against the trunk of the tree.

What should I do? I can't get it to move. Are you climbing up? I called. I felt the vibration again. The rotten branch slid down-wards, and then stopped. I couldn't reach to kick it now. Then I heard the young man calling my name.

Midsummer day, 1927, and choking hot. It was very close up there, surrounded by leaves.

Hello? Rose?

The young man's voice came from nearby.

Where's Adam? I asked.

On the ground. I say, where are you?

I climbed down a few feet and peered through the leafy curtain that hung between us. He looked excited.

Why did you climb up, sir? I said. He was standing on the top rung of the big wooden ladder that I had climbed up an hour previously.

Is your name Rose? he asked me.

Yes, sir, I said. Then, louder, Adam, the branch is going to fall! I called. He waved his end of the rope from down below. He was a local man, middle-aged, consumptive, with a big moustache and belly, too thickabout, as he put it, to be climbing around like a monkey.

Please be careful, sir, I said.

My name's Robbie, he told me, with a nervous smile, extending his hand. I held out my own hand. Stretching towards me he overbalanced. The ladder teetered, then came back upright. Instead of resting against the trunk of the tree, the top of the ladder lay against one of the horizontal branches. As we shook hands, the ladder began to slide along the branch.

Adam shouted and lumbered forward, but he was too far away to reach the ladder in time. It was going to topple.

And then, with a noise like tearing cotton jersey, the rotten branch slipped through the tangle of foliage. Adam had let go of his end of the rope, so that, instead of being lowered gently, the branch fell heavily to the ground, the rope streaming after it like a banner.

Robbie gave no sign of being in danger. He smiled charmingly — an amazing full-mouthed smile — and kept hold of my hand. My indrawn breath stuck in my throat. I choked in admiration. Nice to meet you, Rose; I'm Robbie Rolyoke, he said. Using my hand to guide him, he leapt nimbly onto the branch as the ladder, twenty-five feet of solid hardwood, slid away from us and dropped with a twisting crack right on top of the fallen branch.

Rolyoke? I said. I mean, Mr. Rolyoke, sir?

My dad's Mr. Rolyoke, he told me. I'm just Robbie.

I watched the wreckage from above, peering down through the hole in my refuge, fascinated, distanced, safe.

Harriet's smile is not charming. There there, Mother, she says.

Feeling better then now, dear? asks the woman on the other side of the bed. What do you call her. Suitcase?

Hello, I say.

Where were you, Mother?

I look around the room. Four beds, including mine. My daughter. A ... not suitcase. Nurse. What d'you mean, where was I? I say. I was here. Wasn't I?

I look at my hands. Sometimes I can tell where I've been from them.

I've been here all along, I say.

I wonder, says Harriet. You seemed a long way away.

We're back, though, aren't we? says the ... nurse.

I smile up at her, a motherly woman with an accent from Scotland. I was never motherly enough. And I've never been to Scotland. I start to cry. I'm crying because I've never been to Scotland.

Now, now, says the nurse. That'll not help us, will it, dear?

I try to tell them.

I'm sorry, I say to Harriet.

There there, she says.

So, do you play cards? he asked me.

No, I said.

Do you ride?

Not really, I said. We had a horse but he died.

Any beaux?

I looked away.

Forgive me, he said. I didn't mean to pry. I just ... what do you do for fun, then, Rose?

I stared at him, Robbie Rolyoke, Lady Margaret's son, a nervous excited young man sitting next to me in midair. Our hands on the branch above were very close together.

I don't know, I said.

He understood, I think. He nodded. His face was red. Sweat trickled down into his collar.

It was sunny, the first time Harriet took me to the doctor's office. The first time it was sunny. The next few times it was rainy. The first time the sun made my eyes hurt. She helped me up the steps. Why are we here? I asked. I'd been asking all morning. I'm not sick, I said. For the first time in months I wasn't sick. I was all better. I'd had a bad cold, at least I think it was a cold, lots of coughing. No one thought to take me to the doctor when I was coughing. Not me, not Harriet. Not Robbie. Well, Robbie was dead. Mama was dead too. Doctors are busy people — no point in bothering them, she always said. But I was better now, finally, and now Harriet was taking me to the doctor.

Why are we here? I asked again. This time we were in the feather duster — I mean the waiting room. Harriet made a face and told me to shush. I looked around the room and saw a roomful of long faces and trembly limbs.

Harriet looked angry. Don't do that, Mother, she told me. What was I doing, I wonder. My hands were clean, but she wiped them anyway. The sun was making me blink. I got up to close the curtains. Harriet was talking to another lady, whose mom was fidgeting and crying. Poor thing, sitting in the ... I swallowed. Come back, Harriet called.

I frowned back at her from the hallway. Wonder what I was doing there. Just getting a drink, I told her.

She came to get me. Wiped my hands. They were a little dirty now. Don't do that, she told me. The sno-cone called Harriet's name.

That's what she looked like — white uniform, tapered down from the shoulders, cherry-coloured hair. Harriet Rolyoke? And Rose? The doctor will see you now.

I stood up and walked all by myself. You look just like a sno-cone, I told her, beaming. She didn't say anything. Probably used to that. I'm eighty-six years old, I told her. Proudly. And I don't know why I'm here.

The doctor couldn't see me. Hello, I told him, waving, but he kept talking to Harriet. When did your mother start to forget things? he asked.

Now that's a stupid question, isn't it? I've been forgetting things for years, ever since I can remember. And why ask Harriet? She doesn't know. She doesn't live with me. She comes over to turn off things I've left on and read me the news. I'm the one forgetting things. Why not ask me. Hello, doctor, I said. He pointed his teeth at me but kept looking at Harriet. All those years I tried to get men interested in her, to no avail. It's finally worked. The doctor is infatuated. A good-looking man too, soft curly hair and dark skin. Too bad Harriet's over sixty. And bossy. And, please forgive a mother's honesty, not really beautiful.

Are you Jewish? I asked the doctor. He looked through me, nodded to Harriet. I guess he was saying yes.

Harriet was embarrassed. Please be quiet, Mother. You asked that the last time you came here, she said.

Oh, I said. Thinking, So this isn't my first visit to Dr. Sylvester — there, I remembered the name at last. Does that sound Jewish? All I remember of the Old Testament is what we had to learn in Sunday School, and I don't remember any Sylvester.

It was sunny, that day. I'm sure.

He gave me a test. Harriet left the room and I was all alone with the handsome doctor. Not a pinprick, pee-into-this, breathe-into-that kind of test; this was question and answer. I had to smile, the questions were so silly. *In what way are an egg and a seed alike?* He stared at me as he asked this, so concerned.

Eat them both for breakfast, I told him.

He wanted more. *Why are dark-coloured clothes warmer than light-coloured clothes?*

Seriously, like this had an answer. Do I look like a fashion designer? I said to him.

Or, *What should you do if while in the movies you were the first to see smoke and fire?*

Depends, I said.

On what?

On whether it's a tragedy or a comedy, I told him. If it's a comedy, you can laugh. The doctor, now I've forgotten his name again, got a bit upset. This is serious, he said. If it's a serious movie, I guess you can worry, I said.

I was getting hungry but he didn't offer me anything to eat. What he did was start saying numbers. 5, 9, 4, he said. I smiled politely. He waited. You're supposed to repeat them, he said.

Repeat what, I asked.

The numbers I just gave you.

Why? I asked.

Because we're trying to determine how good your memory is, he told me. It's a test.

I've never been very good at numbers. I remember my daughter being incredulous at how I kept my books at the flower shop. It comes of not ever learning how to subtract, you see. I don't like to tell people, but it's the truth. I must have skipped that part of my schooling. I'm very good at adding up; if a customer bought a dozen long-stemmed roses and a bouquet of fresh-cut flowers for his girlfriend I would be able to tot them up — $6.99 for the roses and $8.00 for the flowers — and tell him that he owed me whatever it was. I could even make change from the twenty-dollar bill. But I could never figure out the difference between what I paid for things and what I got from the people who bought them. Why I didn't go bankrupt I'll never know. Maybe I did go bankrupt and never noticed.

They say poverty marks you, that you never really get over being poor. I think that's true, but not only about money. What do You think — sorry, there I go again, You don't think anything. You know. Well, I have been poor in spirit, poor in love, and that has marked me. Forgive me, I loved Harriet as well as I could. Better than I was loved as a girl.

Goodbye, Mama, I said from the doorway of our house on Forth Street in Cobourg. She didn't answer, she wasn't there. I would have been seventeen, conscious of my uniform, of the picture on the mantel in the parlour, our only memento of Daddy. I didn't want Mama around when I said goodbye. I didn't know what she thought of goodbyes, of our new house, of me. I didn't know her. Poor in spirit. Mr. Davey was waiting outside to drive me to the train station. A brilliant fall day, leaves whirling down the street in fragrant clouds of colour. Me and Miss Parker spent it in the train, Cobourg to New York to Philadelphia. She knitted, and criticized whatever I was doing. I read for a while, then gazed out the window and thought about a place with a million people all living together. A huge place, bigger than a thousand Precious Corners. It boggled my mind. In the movies you saw cities a block at a time — except for ancient Babylon. I couldn't imagine a real city, full of real people. Sit straight, Rose, said Parky. Don't gawp and roll your eyes, anyone would think you were a halfwit.

First person I saw in Philadelphia was dark skinned. So was the second. I would have stared; you didn't see a lot of dark-skinned people in Cobourg. Next thing I remember, the whole platform was full of people. I followed Parky's wide skirts.

The Rolyokes lived in Rittenhouse Square, in a huge L-shaped house with a tower at the top and a curving driveway at the bottom. It wasn't the biggest place on the square any more, but it had been when Mr. Rolyoke's dad built it out of textiles. That's what Robbie told me, later. I don't understand how fortunes are made. Other houses in the neighbourhood were built out of oil, and coal, and railways, and at least one, it was rumoured, was built out of liquor.

At first I lived in the tower with the other girls. You remember my room, the one I shared with Jane. We could see the river from the window. Becky and Mrs. Porson lived across the hall. She wasn't a girl, Mrs. Porson, but her husband was dead and she was just kitchen help so she had to share. Miss Parker lived underneath. If one of us girls got up in the middle of the night, Parky knew about it. There wasn't a bathroom, of course, and I remember clamping my legs together to keep from having to use the chamber pot under my bed. There's a trick to that, you know — clasp your left ankle under your right heel and lock your two knees straight. Works every time — every time. Becky never got the hang of it; she kept wetting her bed. She was a really pretty girl, but nervous. She cried. She didn't last long. Jane was different. Parky didn't bother her the way she did me, because she knew Jane was tougher than I was — hell, she was tougher than Parky herself. She had a way of looking at you if there was something she didn't want to do. Her expression would say something like, You'll have to kill me before you can make me do This. Even if This was washing the floor. And Parky knew that look was there — and so I spent a lot of time washing the floor. Maybe it was because Jane was dark skinned. I never asked her about it. She didn't encourage intimacy. I never heard why she left. I told her I was homesick, the first week I was there, missing Mama and the places I knew. Jane looked up at me, short dark woman with muscles under hard flesh, hair slicked down tight, and looked away.

I have no idea, I said to the handsome doctor. Numbers are so hard to hang on to, I said. Like watermelon seeds — you try to pick them up and they slip through your fingers. I couldn't tell you the numbers forward, let alone backward. He wrote something down, then smiled and told me a story about a woman named Helen going to the supermarket. I tried to pay attention, but nothing much happened to Helen — no conflict at the frozen foods, no hold-up at the cash register — and my mind wandered.

Lady Margaret was staring at a bowl of flowers on a small table in the brown drawing room. Beautiful, she said — to herself? She was alone, I mean, I was in the room but I was used to not being there. People talked but not to me. I didn't say anything, bent my head and kept dusting, maybe blushed a bit. Lady Margaret backed up and bumped into me.

Rose, she said. She smiled. I ducked my head.

Are you getting along all right, dear?

Yes, ma'am. I mean milady.

Miss Parker giving you lots to do?

Yes. I couldn't help wincing.

She's a very experienced manager. And so talented. Isn't this a beautiful flower arrangement she's made?

Would it have been a test? I'd made the arrangement, of course; I made the arrangements every morning in the conservatory.

I'm glad you like it, I said.

Becky came in then, curtseyed to Lady Margaret and said I was wanted in the kitchen. Lady Margaret smiled and told me I could go. I followed Becky with my heart full of dread.

You don't remember any of the story? The doctor looked puzzled, his dark eyes all soft and full of moisture. I don't know why he was concerned, it wasn't much of a story. Something about Helen, I said. I think she was worried. She didn't want to go back to the kitchen with her cantaloupe. I shuddered.

Mrs. Rolyoke.

That's me. I looked up, into the doctor's face. He handed me a tissue.

Do you know what we're doing here this morning? he asked. We're trying to find out about your health. Your daughter is concerned.

I know, I said.

You're forgetting a lot of things, he said. Now, we all forget some things, that's normal, but you're forgetting things you should remember. Things that might be dangerous. The physical tests we gave you last time didn't tell us much. Now I'm giving you these little memory tests. The story about Helen and the supermarket is one of them. We see how much you remember now, and then how much you remember in ten minutes. We're measuring the rate of memory loss. Do you understand?

He was starting to sound agitated. There there, I told him.

But you see, Mrs. Rolyoke, you don't remember anything now. How can I measure your rate of memory loss, if we start at zero?

Yes, I said.

It was the same with the numbers. You didn't get them confused when you said them backward, you didn't get them at all.

Yes, I said.

Mrs. Rolyoke, do *you* think you're forgetting things? He stared at me. This was an important question. Of course, I said. I'd forget my hands if they weren't attached to my smokestacks. I mean arms, I said. I smiled. He was so handsome.

And now let me ask *you* something, I said.

He sighed. Was I giving the wrong answer again?

Are you married? I asked.

Robbie and I were married in Philadelphia, in a little Episcopalian church off Juniper Street with no one there except Mr. Rolyoke and Mama and Bill Scanlon, her husband. I wouldn't have minded calling him Daddy, but he told me to call him Bill. He was a straight-shooting kind of guy, from the Maritimes originally, who volunteered with the Cobourg firefighters and worked in the Bank of Commerce where Mama deposited her employer's savings.

Robbie and I met them at the train station. Mama was pleased for me, and not pleased, both at the same time. You've done well, haven't you, she said, very quietly, so the dark-skinned porter wouldn't hear. I burst into tears. Mama was in her best dress, with gloves and a shawl. She took Robbie's arm and went on about his family. He smiled weakly and said, How do you do. He and Bill nodded to each other. Lovely day, Bill said. We had a cab waiting and Mama told the porter to put their luggage into it.

The minister stammered out our names, and spent the whole service looking at Mr. Rolyoke's morning coat. My father-in-law seemed remote, unapproachable, and somehow all-powerful.

Robbie was charming and happy, smiled at me, made jokes that no one laughed at. He didn't bring a best man, so we used Bill. Hope you don't mind marrying the second-best man, he told me. Mama kept looking around from the front row. The church was empty, except for Mr. Davey at the back, his chauffeur's cap on the pew beside him.

Mr. Rolyoke gave me away. I remember the pressure of his hand on my arm. Gentle, reassuring. Do not fear, he murmured to me. I guess I was shaking. His expression was impossible for me to read through my veil. He wasn't happy, or sad, or angry. He just was.

We had the wedding breakfast at a hotel and then took the train north. I didn't eat much, say much, do much. I would have been feeling a little sickly by then. Not every day, but most of them. My new blue dress fit wonderfully, flattering my hips and hiding my tummy. And there was a surprise in the pocket, a last-minute wedding gift from Mr. Rolyoke. I didn't discover it until it was too late to thank him.

And so, with the summer ending around us, in an atmosphere of anxiety and cigar smoke, we went to Niagara Falls. The hotel room looked northwest, and the view of the sun setting behind the horseshoe falls through the light feathery clouds was everything the picture postcards promised, and in colour too. Made me shiver, and catch my breath. I sent postcards to Gert and her sisters, and my other friends in Cobourg. I hoped they hadn't moved since I was there last. I would have sent one to Mama, but I didn't think she wanted to hear from me.

Later that night Robbie told funny stories about horseback riding to cheer me up. He wore a shiny dressing gown with those clasps on the front, frogs, is that it? And leather slippers. He had a flask of bootleg whisky, but he put it on the bedside table after a couple of drinks. His bed had a blue spread — mine was wine coloured.

I'm sorry about your mother, I said.

He stared at me. So am I, he said.

I never knew she could be so mean, I said.

He didn't say anything. Maybe he did know. I'd never seen the two of them together, exchanging secrets, telling jokes, being close. He laughed when he was amused, she only smiled in a pained sort of way, as if being amused was a chore. And they weren't amused by the same things.

Do you think you'll ever see her again? I was asking about his mother but thinking about Mama. Would I ever see her again?

Not if she sees me first, he said. But I'll see you, Rose, every day. And in a few months I'll see the baby. Tell you what: Let's move away from Philadelphia. Just the three of us. We'll get a jolly little place somewhere and let mother stew in her own juice. Forget about her. Right after the honeymoon, we'll get on a train or boat, or we'll buy a car and just drive. What do you think, Rose? Where would you like to live?

I was a girl, married only that day to a man I hardly knew well, a man I'd served, whose world and way of living were different from mine. How many of the same things did we know? I was two months pregnant. I didn't know what I wanted to eat right then, let alone where I wanted to live for the rest of my life.

You decide, I said.

All right, I will.

The sun was long gone. There were torches and gas lamps in the streets below our room. I was tired. He helped me into bed. Thank you, I said.

For what?

You know, I said. He blew me a kiss and climbed into his own bed.

In the morning the waiter brought us tea and toast in our room. Robbie thanked him warmly. I thanked him too.

Where you folks from? he said. Don't sound like you're from New York.

Where do we sound like we're from? Robbie asked.

The waiter thought a bit. Sound kind of foreign, he said. Like English or something. Had a couple here the other day, sounded like you. They was from Toronto. You know Toronto?

Robbie and I looked at each other. Know it? said Robbie. That's where we're from.

Thought so, said the waiter. You sound like it.

He touched his little hat, closed the door gently behind him.

Three days later we arrived at Union Station. Robbie asked where the best hotel was and was directed across the street to the Royal York. The porter who wheeled our bags was surprised by the size of his tip. You folks not from around here, are you, he said, respectfully.

We are now, I said.

We didn't live at the hotel for long. I was unsure of myself, unused to deference, luxury, having material wants gratified. It would have been just after we'd found a house, maybe a month after our arrival in Toronto, that the stock market crashed.

I have so much regret in me. You know that. You were there. Course You were. You saw me being beaten by that crazy Miss Parker. Not clean enough, the floor, the cooker, the pots — and me on my knees, sobbing. Not clean enough! I hated You so much.

I know I should be understanding, accepting, forgiving of my enemies — but it was hard to forgive, there in the back kitchen. Even now I can feel the hard cool flags under my knees — I used to count them as I waited for the next blow to fall.

Rose, my dear, what's the matter? That was her — Lady Margaret. I'd be wincing, carrying a plate into the dining room. I didn't want to be there at all, not with my sore back. But Lady Margaret insisted. I want to see how you're doing, my dear, she'd tell me. We both do. With a glance at Mr. Rolyoke.

I'm fine, milady, I would say. Fine.

That's good.

But I wasn't fine. The old sailors' rhyme says that when the wind follows the sun, fine weather will never be done, but in my life the wind had shifted against the sun, and I trusted it not, for back it would run. More than once, with my back smarting, I thought about giving notice, but I knew I'd never get another position without a reference. And I couldn't bear the idea of Mr. Rolyoke not approving of me. He was such a gentleman, quiet and grave, full of important thoughts. I've never had any of those. My mind wanders off, like a dog in a park full of strange scents. He was considerate too. When I accidentally brushed against the bowl of his pipe he was more concerned for my burnt arm than the crystal brandy snifter I'd dropped. Next morning at breakfast Parker beat me with a wooden spoon because the milk for the porridge wasn't hot enough. Any hotter and it would have scalded, I told her, and she beat me harder. Sitting in the high wooden chair this time, arms folded to protect my breasts.

You're frowning. Should I have done something? Run away, fought back, told Lady Margaret? You're shaking Your head. Should I have *not* done something?

I loved the conservatory, early in the morning. The row of vases on one of the long benches, the moist warm air, the quiet. Parker tried to criticize my work, but even she knew it was something I could do better than anyone else there.

After a big and successful party Lady Margaret took one of my best arrangements into the kitchen and tore it to pieces, stem by stem, running the stems through her nails, crushing the blossoms into juice. We'd already been sent to bed; I wasn't supposed to be there, but I watched from behind the door, fascinated. The look on her face was one of intense rage.

Maybe the party hadn't been such a success. I hurried up to my bedroom. I would have been alone by now, in the room beside Parker's. Sometimes I could hear her grunting in her sleep.

Robbie's face was round, pale, fleshy, with always a faint sheen of sweat near the surface. His eyes bulged faintly behind the glasses. His brown hair, parted neatly on the left and brushed backwards, never seemed to grow. He was enthusiastic and vague at the same time; he'd come back to the hotel all excited about a great house he'd seen, it'd suit us to the ground, big kitchen and living room, great view of the park, and a nursery for the baby — only he'd be unable to remember the address. Or the location. Which park? I'd ask. Could you see the lake? Was it on a hill? West or east of Yonge Street — you remember Yonge Street, I'd tell him — the big street with all the theatres? He'd smile, shake his head, and laugh at himself. It was an eighty-cent cab ride, he'd say.

I got in touch with a real estate agent, an old sourpuss with those big ears that really old skinny-headed people get. Remember how excited he was when he found out our name. Any relation to the textile company? he asked. And when Robbie nodded, he said, You know the stock just hit eighteen dollars a share. Tell me — do you think it's due to split again? September, this would have been. Robbie giggled and said he had no idea. We called the real estate office after we moved into the house on Waverley, to ask something about taxes, but the phone had been disconnected.

The voice rattles in my ear, like a key in the locked door of my prison cell. I wonder what he's saying. His arms are in front of him, gesturing. Like he's praying. He looks worried, great blisters of sweat on his face. Harriet nods in earnest agreement. Hospitals are so military, like battleships of caring. This guy will be an officer of sorts. He points at me, points at Harriet, makes his gesture again. He looks earnest but he sounds like a shovel full of gravel.

My daughter is wearing a beautiful dress. I didn't know she had one like it, quite takes me back to another era. I'm in bed, lying down. I want to sit up but can't. My head feels heavy and my arms are as weak as a baby's. My daughter is holding my hand.

What does that mean? says my daughter. I perk up. I can understand her. The rest of the noises that filter through the world to me are meaningless, but I know her voice. My daughter is speaking, and I can understand what she is saying.

I squeeze her hand.

She spares a moment to look down at me.

Harriet, I say. She doesn't respond.

Harriet. I say it louder. Harriet Harriet. Do you hear me?

She pats my hand. How much time do we have? she says.

She's not talking to me. She can't understand me.

The man says something. A white uniform, very formal — what is he, a doctor? He doesn't look particularly medical. Not like my nice Dr. Sylvester. There was a man, now. What large dark eyes, like two of Ali Baba's oil jars. Deep, rich, shiny, fattening — oh, to have eyes like that. To marry eyes like that. To be able to stare into them whenever you liked.

A simple test, Dr. Sylvester said, giving me a cardboard clock with movable hands. Big hand, little hand. I thought of all the hands, withered old hands like mine, clutching the little cardboard hands of the clock. I thought of all the old men and women like me, trying to understand what the doctor was asking us to do. Trying to do what we were told because it was important to someone — not to us. Certainly not to me; I've never been any good at telling what time it was.

Once a policeman came in to buy flowers, and said I'd have to go to court because the store was open too late.

And what time is it anyway? I asked. I've no head for the hours, they just fly by.

It's well after six o'clock, missus, he said, pointing to his wrist-watch. Too late, he said.

Too late for what? I asked.

Too late for the men that write the laws downtown, he said.

He'd come in with a smile and a kind word, bought carnations for his wife and waited for me to wrap them, then pulled out the summons. Piece of paper.

How'd you know to come here? I asked.

Neighbour complaint, he said, writing busily. Friendly fat policeman with a moustache and a well-licked pencil.

Who? Which neighbour? I had my suspicions — this was still wartime, most people were worried about Hitler, not extra-hours businesses. Was it the guy from the BP station on the corner? I asked.

The policeman handed me the summons.

It was, wasn't it, I said.

He reached into his jacket pocket and found an apple. Took a deliberate bite.

That bastard, I said. Just because he can't sell gas after six.

Harriet had been doing her homework in the back room. She came into the shop as the policeman left, taking the flowers with him.

When's dinnertime? she asked. I'm starving.

I didn't say anything.

What's wrong? She recognized the summons in my hand. Is that why the policeman was here? Are we open too late again, Mother? We are, aren't we.

What time is it? I asked.

What's going to happen? Remember what the judge said last time?

That bastard McIntosh, I said.

Don't swear, Mother. Do you mean Mr. McIntosh? From the gas station? Has he been complaining again?

Is it really after six o'clock? I said.

We were standing in the door of the shop. A cold clear winter evening. She pointed to the tower on the firehall across the street. I could just make out the hands on the big clock.

It's practically seven, Mother — see?

Not really, I said.

Are you finished? Dr. Sylvester asked me very gently. I guess I'd been staring into space for a while.

Ten past eleven, right? I said, frowning down at the bent and withered clock hands, at my own hands, which weren't withered at all but lumpy — great bumps of chalk and bone that rear up suddenly, like volcanoes from the earth's crust.

I might have set it at ten past eleven. That's the time he wanted me to do. Does that say ten past eleven? I asked him.

He smiled kindly. I don't think he hated me — probably on account of my profile. He must have a tough life, though, shepherding thousands of uncertain old people through the Gates of Ivory. Watching their minds curl up at the edges like drying paper. Knowing that every time he saw them they'd be farther and farther away — and they'd never get better. None of them. Who'd be him? Mind you, who'd be me? Who'd be anybody if they could help it?

Dr. Sylvester shook his head kindly and put the clock away. End of the test for today. We'll do some more another time, he said, writing something in my file. Probably not about my cheekbones, though they had been praised in their day.

Was that the reason behind McIntosh's accusation, do you think? Was he truly in love with me? That's what Harriet said, but what did she know? A little girl with geometry homework, what would she know about true love? He was an ordinary-looking man, middle-aged, middle-sized, hair that was neither brown nor black nor grey, but sort of a blend of them all. His chin was kind of long, and his nose was high-bridged. He had very short eyebrows — they only went halfway across his face, which meant he always looked a bit taken aback.

Why did you call the cops on me? I asked him, the day after my summons. He was in the store to buy flowers. Loved flowers, he said, but had no one to give them to. Over the grime of years, his hands were red and raw with washing. The nails were clean.

What do you mean, Rose? he asked. He had a high, soft voice.

Last night a policeman came to my shop and charged me with operating after hours, I said. He was tipped off by a neighbour.

Why do you think it was me?

It was you last time, I said.

He looked down at his boots. Neither of us had mentioned the last time.

How do you know it wasn't that guy from the bakery?

Geoff?

Yes. Geoff.

His eyes darkened on the name. Not that Geoff Zimmerman and I were anything more than friendly acquaintances. His bakery stood between the hardware store and Ruby's hat shop, about a block east of my flower shop. I bought my bread and baked goods at Geoff's place. If he was there, he waited on me himself, a bear of a guy, handsome and hairy, with a habit of looking away from you when he talked. Looking away from me anyway.

Mr. McIntosh bought some gardenias and hesitated at the door. Why don't I give them to you, Rose? he asked.

Because they're already mine, I said. If I take them back, all you've given me is money.

Would this have been my first winter in the shop? My second? I felt pretty damn lonely. Mr. McIntosh tried to be sympathetic. What a fine man your husband must have been, he said. I'm so sorry I never got a chance to meet him.

Thanks, I said quietly, and had to repeat myself. Mr. McIntosh was hard of hearing, the reason he wasn't fighting in Europe.

Robbie's fighting had all been in the Atlantic. There's a picture of him somewhere, in his blue uniform smoking a cigarette. And another one of the ship — not a boat, there's a difference — getting swamped. I remember Robbie and Harriet laughing over that picture, but it made me scared the moment I saw it.

Good luck, Robbie, wherever you are.

No one knows exactly how senile dementia works, Dr. Sylvester told Harriet. I was there for another test, I think. Wellesley — that can't be right. That was Ruby's name. Ruby Wellesley Millinery, it said over her shop. Anyway there was a whole series of these tests to prove that I was really losing my mind. Unnecessary. They could just have asked me. Rose Rolyoke, are you losing your mind? I'd have been able to tell them all right. Saved a lot of trouble.

Harriet frowned intently as the doctor talked, every now and then turning to look at me with the strangest mixture of compassion and exasperation. Reminded me of the time I found her in court, after I'd lost her.

Yes, she said to the doctor. She thinks of that often.

Thinks about what, I wondered.

It must have been traumatic, the doctor said.

Harriet gave me the look again.

My father died a violent death. I didn't witness it, but I heard about it at the trial. Uncle Brian didn't hide anything; he was still too upset. They'd been out hunting moose in the Ganaraska Forest, he and Daddy. After a no-luck day they were passing an evening with a bottle of Mr. McAllister's rotten whisky, when a bull moose wandered right up to the edge of their campfire and began nibbling at a blueberry bush. The men scrambled to get their guns and fired from point-blank range. Uncle Brian described how the moose stared at them calmly with one big wet eye, while the blood poured out of the wound in his side. Made me feel guilty inside, to see the suffering in the dumb animal, he said. But apparently Daddy got excited — strange for him, who never seemed to care about anything. He kept firing, even after the moose turned and loped off. Reminded me of what happened to Victor.

Daddy said he wanted the moosehead for the house. Come on, Brian, he called, reloading his gun, grabbing the axe and plunging into the brush after the animal. Brian stopped for a last drink, and followed the sound of my father's passage through the underbrush, heard a shot, and then another, and couldn't locate them. He wandered around, then sat down and slept for a while, and dreamed about a crowd of men nailing the moose to a cross — like the moose was Jesus, he told the judge, who told him to go on — and the sound of the hammering got louder and louder and finally woke Uncle Brian from his sleep, sweating and crying out. The hammering was real. The sound of the blows echoed through the forest. Uncle Brian sprang to his feet, lost in the woods at night, and afraid. The noise was coming from dead ahead of him.

The moon was near full, and it was possible to pick his way with care. Uncle Brian described to the court how he walked. Like a Red Indian, he said, careful not to let a twig snap under my boots, and the beating of my heart was all mixed up with the pounding noise ahead of me. It was like I was listening to the heartbeat of the forest, he said, and the judge told him to please get to the point.

The noise stopped, and the forest was silent and still. Uncle Brian kept walking, hardly daring to breathe. And then, treading silently as they do, rearing high above him, was the moose, huge spread of antlers clearly silhouetted in the moonlight. The beast was upon him in an instant. He fired instinctively, in self-defence — the moose being capable of derailing a freight train, as he explained. Only of course it wasn't a moose. It was my father, labouring along with the moose's head on his shoulders — the head he had with so much labour hacked off with his axe.

If Daddy had been a moose, Uncle Brian's shot would have taken him high on the foreleg, near the shoulder, a crippling blow. But with the extra four feet of head and antlers on top of his own head, the solid shot — no pellets for Uncle Brian — hit Daddy square in the throat. People aren't horses; there are lots of places you can hit them so that they die fast. Daddy died instantly.

Dog spoon laughter edge quarterback, said Dr. Sylvester, in a nice wool suit. I beg your pardon? I asked. I assumed I'd heard wrong, but no, it was part of the test.

He repeated them, and then wanted me to say them back. I cleared my throat, something sticking there from breakfast, and repeated them flawlessly. I've always been able to do that. Song lyrics too. Remember Minnie the Moocher? Hi-de-hi-de-hi-de-hi?

The past is always knocking on the door of the present, said Dr. Sylvester, this time in a nice linen suit. Was he talking to me? A pleasant image that, only the past isn't always polite. Sometimes it knocks the damn door down and comes barging in.

I believe, said the doctor, that the past cannot be suppressed without cost. In wilfully suppressing the past we are living two lives at once — our real life and a fantasy life where the past hasn't happened. Do you follow?

He wasn't talking to me. Harriet nodded.

As we get older our minds lose their agility. We can no longer keep the past out of the present. And so, in people like your mother, past and present co-exist. Short-term memory gets swallowed up by long-term memory. She is living in the present — but the present is 1927. Or 1912. Rose — he knows my name, how lovely. I smile at him. Rose, what date is it today?

The verdict should have been accidental death, but Uncle Brian felt so guilty. I shot Jesus Christ, he told the court. That's who it was, in the woods, larger than any other animal. I knew what I was doing and I shot Jesus, only it turned out to be my brother. I deserve to die, he moaned. If you let me go I'll only do it again.

Mama had tears in her eyes when they led Uncle Brian away, and I knew something important had happened because Mama hadn't cried in years, never did cry but from relief.

Funny how relieved you can feel in a courtroom — I cried too, when I entered the small courtroom in the basement of City Hall. The varnished hall outside was full of smoking women, but it wasn't the smoke that made my eyes water. It was relief at finding her. Not Mama. Harriet. I'm always getting them mixed up.

I showed my yellow summons to three or four different people before someone told me what the trouble was. That's the date of your hearing, said an old tired guard, pointing at the top of the cardboard. The thirteenth. That's tomorrow.

Harriet was ahead of me, pacing up and down the shiny tiled floor in her winter coat and new Christmas galoshes.

Tomorrow, I said to the guard.

Uh huh, he said.

I sighed and called Harriet. I walked slowly out of the big stone building, part of a crowd of preoccupied people. Sleet was coming down, and umbrellas and coat collars were going up. The newspaper boy in front of the cenotaph was shouting about victory in the Ardennes. No empty seats on the streetcar, of course. We stood and swayed on this chilly, soggy, crowded, and totally wasted afternoon while the streetcar jostled its way down Queen Street. Everyone around me was reading war news stories. I got a seed catalogue out of my purse and tried to pay attention to the loveliest words in English, words of hope and glory, of trust that the coming year would bring forth beauty.

Look at this one, Harriet, I said, pointing to a perfectly shaped Dorothy Perkins in, reputedly, a vivid pink. The photograph was black and white, but you could see that the bloom was large and perfectly shaped, petals crisp and curling.

Harriet wasn't beside me. I searched through the strap-hangers while fear rose hot and bitter in my throat. My daughter was not in the streetcar. We were across the Don River already, out of the downtown. Closer to home than City Hall. The bathwater flooded over the sides of my mind. I had left without my daughter. I had no mental picture, no actual memory of Harriet's departure from City Hall. I leaned over to pull the call-stop bell.

Dr. Sylvester was interested in my actual memory, my ability to make pictures in my head. I'm going to tell you a story, he said once. I don't know what kind of suit he was wearing, which visit this would have been. Harriet wasn't in the room. I smiled because I loved stories. Still do.

This one ended and I thanked the doctor. He asked me what I thought and I told him the truth, that I was very glad he'd taken the time to tell me the story. You're a busy man, I said with my fluffy wide smile, and old people like me like to hear stories from the world outside. I live in an apartment now, I told him, and I don't get out much. He frowned, wanted to hear more about the story. How much did I actually remember? he asked. Did I have any mental pictures?

I remember the first time I held a man in my arms, I said. I can close my eyes and see the moonlight playing on the muscles of his back. A cold winter moon. We lay in a castle overlooking the river, and he was kind and good and mysterious to me.

Dr. Sylvester's frown deepened.

The westbound streetcar, taking me back to City Hall, was almost empty. I can feel the swaying carriage, feel the hard wooden back of the seat next to mine. I stared out the window to the right, and left, in case Harriet had decided to walk home by herself. The driver called out the stops — Church Street, Victoria, Yonge, Bay Street — and then I was running through the still-falling rain, up the worn slippery stone steps, looking for someone to tell my story to, a uniformed someone who would lead me away from the crowds to a quiet room where my daughter would be sitting safely, waiting for me.

No one had seen her. No one knew her. The lost and found was full of old hats. I began to cry.

The lady in charge of the lost and found had a hump on her shoulder and dyed blonde hair. She looked at my summons. I suppose you've tried your hearing room, she said. I shook my head. My hearing isn't until tomorrow, I said. She looked at the yellow cardboard again. The thirteenth is today, she said.

She led me to the basement, down a hallway filled with the smell of cigarette smoke and stale, unwashed, made-up women. The tall, narrow wooden door was closed tight. She put her humped shoulder to it and opened it for me. There was a hearing in progress, judge and official reporter, police witness, and my Harriet on her feet, asking questions. Are you wearing a watch? she asked the fat smiling policeman from last month.

Yes, miss, he said politely.

I turned to thank the lady from the lost and found, but she was gone. The tall door had closed behind her. I took a seat at the back of the room, settling into my relief like sleep, letting it wash over and renew me.

Without looking at your watch, do you know what time it is right now?

Not exactly — not to the minute, miss.

And are you in the habit of checking your watch every minute, officer?

No, miss, but —

Did you check your watch when you were in the flower shop?

Not *while* I was in it, but —

Is there a clock in the flower shop? A visible clock? Anywhere in the store.

No, miss.

So you don't know what time it was, when you were in the shop. Not to the minute.

No, miss. Not to the minute. But it was plainly past six o'clock.

Then why, officer, if it was plainly past six o'clock, did you buy flowers yourself, while you were in the store?

I watched the smile grow on the judge's face. He didn't try to hide it.

Did you take the flowers home, officer? Harriet asked the policeman.

Why, uh, no, miss. I gave them to a ... to a friend that night.

Did your friend like the flowers?

Yes, miss, she did.

The policeman was smiling too. He enjoyed answering my daughter's questions. He liked her as much as the judge did.

Harriet was on her feet. She always wandered around as she talked. Her hands were in the pockets of her skirt. Her hair was plaited, and hung below her shoulders. The braided brown strands swung back and forth as she walked.

Tell me, officer, were you on time for your date?

The policeman's smile broadened. To tell the truth, miss, I was late.

I guess you didn't check your watch, officer. Hmm?

With smiles and handshakes, on grounds that the evidence was inconclusive, the case was dismissed. The judge got down off his chair and held open the door at the back of the room for Harriet. Buy this young lady a treat, he ordered me. And get yourself a clock.

You stride through time like Your living room, but it's dark, and I'm scared. Sick people go in the middle watches, they say. Two, three o'clock in the morning — a busy time for You. It's so dark. I'm glad I'm in my mama's arms.

2

Christmas

A cold bed in a cold house. Even in summer, even at the height of summer when the sweat ran off our bodies and into the ground, into our clothes, into the coarse sack sheets we put on the beds — even then it was a cold house. I shivered, getting out of my sweat-crusted bed. Shivered, on my way to give Victor a big hug. Climbing up on the side of his stall to put my arms around his great shaggy neck. Smell of a hot barn in summer, old hay and wood floor, mice and flies and hot horse.

And I so cold.

Daddy scared me, with his talk that didn't make sense. Mama tried, I think, but she had no time for me. A wan sometimes-smile would live on the surface of her lips for a second or two, a troubled shadow when I wanted a bright blaze of love. Poor Mama. Poor Daddy. Poor me.

And then David came. A sunny youth, a soldier from Daddy's battalion. He was younger than Daddy, of course, a young man with crinkled dark hair and a dimple near the corner of his mouth. Hello, there, he said, rising from the middle of the row of rusty lettuces I was trying to care for. Hello. That was the first time I saw him. His uniform was tattered but somehow clean. I knew it was clean. He was such a clean young man. What is your name? he asked me. I told him, mentioning that my father had been in The War.

We didn't have to wonder which war, back then. There was only one war. Nowadays I hear people saying, Which war do you mean? As if it matters, which one.

Nice to meet you, Rose, David told me. Dusting the knees of his ragged battledress trousers, tucking in the puttees that were always coming unwound.

You are beautiful, I told him. He ducked his head shyly, no doubt used to being told. And let me lead him into the house.

It made me warm, to think of him in the same place as me. Walking out in the fields with me, cleaning out Victor's stall, weeding that damned — sorry, undamned — vegetable patch. Are there weeds in heaven? Flowers I think of, but a weed is only a flower with no admirers, a pretty girl perhaps, but unmoneyed, unknown, and so she sits at the edge of the dance floor, waiting to be asked. Shepherd's parsley, cudweed, ox-eye daisies — I'd like to see them in heaven. But not the creepers and stinkers in our vegetable patch. How I hated them.

David didn't say much. I didn't let him. But he was sunburnt and helpful, and he had a crooked smile. And while the rake and hoe fell with dull strokes on the hard earth, he told me about machine-gun nests and barbed wire and trench rats. He let me give him water from our well, in a sweating pitcher. He let me sponge his aching back, sitting in a kitchen dapple of sunshine. He let me take him with me, to school, to work, to bed. He was my warmth, David Lawrence Godwin.

I borrowed his last name from the side of a van that clattered slowly through Precious Corners in the spring of that year, 1919 I guess it would have been, selling coffin wood that was to have been shipped off to France if The War hadn't ended. Genuine Patriot Wood by Jack Godwin. I don't think too many people bought the elm planks, even though they were cheaper than firewood. I stared at the van clattering by — an event, all right — and the next day in school when I thought about my hero, his name — David Lawrence, his friends in the platoon had always called him Dave, but he liked it that I called him David — became David Lawrence Godwin.

The smudged white pages of my exercise book filled up with our doings. We went riding; David's prowess in the saddle was astonishing. We went fishing; David caught a salmon longer than my arm. And then we went into town. He was admired by all the other women for his looks and his bravery, but he never let go of my arm, the one the salmon was longer than, because deep down he was very shy. And everyone said how lucky I was.

I never thought about his family. At the back of my mind I knew that he had run away to be a soldier. His voice was soft and lilting.

Sometimes I would look up from my plate of stewed pork and greens, into Daddy's empty face, or Mama's anxious one. And feel the cold of the house, as if we were all in the frozen desert huddled around a long-dead fire.

I tried to love them. I tried and tried. But Daddy wouldn't even look at me. His eyes were empty, unless he woke up in the middle of the night screaming, which he did from time to time. And Mama was worried all the time. Sometimes I thought she loved me. Sometimes I thought she would have loved me, but couldn't.

Was I like that? With Harriet, was I like that? I remember her crying in her crib. Running to her, picking her up, and being unable to soothe her. I remember saying, I must love her now. Right now, when I want her to shut up. I must love her.

I tried so hard. Sometimes I think, Love shouldn't be so hard. Love should be easy. But it's not, is it? It's hard. You know.

I wonder if she found it difficult to love me. It must be difficult now. I have difficulty loving me now.

What do You mean, shaking Your head. Why are You looking at me like that? You look like You're about to slap my face the way those stooges do. Am I that stupid? Of course You'd be three stooges in one, wouldn't you. I see the Holy Ghost as Curly. Whoo Whoo Whoo. Now You're smiling.

I couldn't love my parents. I tried, like a dog on a chain, flinging myself against the limit of self. Over and over. And they wouldn't let me come near them. Caring was too dangerous. They might lose — I don't know what they might lose. I wonder why I tried so hard. I wouldn't have been imitating anyone I knew.

They didn't hate me. That came later, from Parker and Lady Margaret. I didn't know how to react. I didn't even know how Lady Margaret felt until that morning in her sitting room. I was so surprised, I stood with my head down, like a silly schoolgirl being bawled out for misconstruing. Which I practically was. A schoolgirl, I mean. I wasn't construing anything at all, so I don't see how I could have been misconstruing.

Parker broke the news with a smile peeking from under her arched eyebrows. Lady M. wanted to see me in the small library. I wonder why, I said. But Parky only waggled her eyebrows and said

I'd soon see. And when I got there she was sitting behind the leather-topped table, staring at a glittering object. I stared too, wondering what it was.

You recognize this then, Rose.

What do you mean?

This. Touching it with the end of her fingernail, as if it might stain.

A cufflink. One of Mr. Robbie's? I said.

When did you see it last?

I don't know, I said.

When?

Don't know.

You lying ignorant strumpet, it was found in your bedroom. It was in your bedroom this morning. He was in your room last night, wasn't he?

My mouth open wide enough to swallow Jonah.

Mr. Robbie? I asked. But how?

Wasn't he?

Mother? The voice changes, still harsh and strident, but without a British accent.

No, I say. Of course he wasn't in my room.

Mother! The voice is shocked. I open my eyes. Harriet, I say. How nice to see you. You lying ignorant strumpet.

Mother, you should rest now.

As opposed to what, I wonder.

The room is not pretty. The walls are the colour of yellow jasmine. What does that mean, now — *sorrow* or *passion*, isn't it? And I can hear the sorrow. Outside of my little curtained world, on the other side of the movable cell wall, is distress. Ladies wailing for their demon lovers? No. Sad little ladies like me, crying while they wait.

But who's this? An elegant young thing, doesn't look more than sixty-five, with just-cut hair and a just-bought suit, smiling professionally. I know her. I wonder who she is. She pulls my curtain shut and stands still, letting me get used to her. I hope she doesn't have a booming voice.

Hello, again, she says.

Oh well.

I'm fine, I say, as quickly as I can. She smiles at me.

The lady across the room is moaning again. Something about her liver. Very nourishing stuff, liver. A bit rich, but good for the blood. No yellow jasmine for her. Barberry — *sharpness of temper*. And laurestine — *I die if neglected*. Silly bitch.

The professional woman pulls a chair up and sits beside me. I know her from somewhere. She takes my hand in hers. Hers is dry and firm, the nails long and well tended. A faint shine to them, like just-dusted furniture. My nails are almost gone, tiny little half moons. Perfectly formed, mind you, smooth-edged blossoms on the end of spidery blue stems.

Hello, there, I tell her. She pats my hand.

Do I know you? I ask.

She keeps patting. She nods her head. Oh dear. Tears trickle down her face.

You're not Ruby, are you? I ask. Or Gert? She shakes her head. Of course not. Gert's exactly my age, our birthdays in the same month. The teacher used to pin flowers to the calendar to mark our birthdays. Primrose, usually, *youth and sadness*, very appropriate. I haven't seen Gert in a long time. And Ruby, my friend from middle age, is dead. I remember now.

Silly me.

That's what Gert used to call me — Silly Rose, she'd say. Dreaming again.

Gert had her family and other friends besides me. She was busy and happy. Even when her sister died of influenza she was happy. Not right away, but soon. She had three more sisters, and a brother. She loved them so much. She didn't spend any time dreaming about warmth. She had it at home.

David Lawrence Godwin was necessary to me. I needed someone to love. So I poured all the love I had — a young girl's love, rich and pure and silly — into him. Even now the picture of his puffed and bruised ankle is enough to draw tears from my eyes. He twisted it, falling off his spirited charger, Destiny.

I don't know where Destiny was supposed to come from. He wasn't there all the time, only when David and I went riding together. I rode Victor, our only horse, neither spirited nor a charger.

David let me take off his boots — you know I don't think he ever changed clothes — and he leaned on me. We walked home slowly together. I have no idea what happened to the horses. I suppose they wandered off. I forgot about them until next time.

I never showed my notebook to anyone.

The pleasant loud-voiced professional woman is still sitting beside my bed, still holding my hand. A patient lady. Are you a nurse? I ask her.

She shakes her head. I try to smile.

Oh, Mother, she says, and turns away.

I knew I'd seen her before.

Miss Parker, round and red-faced, hard-skinned as a nutshell, with a shrivelled rotten soul rattling around inside that starched shirt-front of hers. Miss Parker, who smirked at Lady Margaret and stormed at the rest of us. Parky, we called her, meaning cold, and she was. Even Mr. Davey treated her carefully. Now, Miss Parker, he would say. Try to give Miss Rose a chance.

This after I'd walked into the kitchen with a fork in my mouth. I'd been clearing the great dining room and the stack of dessert plates was slipping and both hands were busy, so I bent instinctively forward — like a dog, Parky said. Actually, she didn't say dog.

I started at Rittenhouse Square as kitchen help, meaning washing up. When there was a specially big party I got to carry into the dining room. Mr. Rolyoke liked me in the dining room. He said I added a splash of grace and beauty. He smiled when I offered him vegetables. Once I didn't take him boiled beets and he called me down the table. I almost burst with confusion.

You didn't offer the dish to me, Rose, he said.

That's because I know you don't like them, sir, I said. I didn't want to embarrass you.

He laughed. It's nice to be able to say no to a pretty girl like you, he told me. The guest on his left, another old man, laughed too.

Lady Margaret didn't seem to hear, but when I offered her some pudding later on she waved it away. Are you not aware, Rose, that I dislike lemon pudding? she asked.

I had to shake my head. No, ma'am, I said, and then blushed again because I knew she liked us to call her milady. Parker always did. I mean no, milady, I murmured, head down, sweat dripping off my nose. Winter outside but warm in the kitchen, with all the ovens going, and I was working hard. Lady Margaret liked the heat on. The radiators used to pop all the time.

I'd been taught to clear properly, right hand into left, but I must have been thinking of something else because the whole stack of dessert plates — mostly empty, Parky made a lovely lemon pudding, one of the few things she understood — slid to one side and I barely caught it in time. Still a dozen steps to the kitchen door. I walked carefully, but a fork was slipping from the top of the stack so I bent down and grabbed it in my teeth, showing up in the kitchen looking like a retriever bitch, as Parky put it.

Mr. Davey was drinking cocoa at the kitchen table, waiting in case one of the guests had trouble with their cars. Not everyone knew how to drive back then. Give Miss Rose a chance, he said, trying to sound calm.

How many more chances does the clumsy cow need? That's not me talking, that was Parky, never circuitous, she always called a spade that bloody thing, as in Get that bloody thing out of my kitchen. She also called me that bloody thing. Go upstairs now, she told me in a throaty whisper so they wouldn't hear in the dining room. You great galoot. You hulking farm girl. I'll pour the coffee myself. Go up to the bedroom — that's where you belong, you — well, You know what she said. With such a glittering leer in her face, a hurt angry jealous passion I couldn't begin to understand.

What did she mean by it? I wasn't that kind of girl. I never was. I knew about sex of course, you can't live a spring in the country and not know what goes on. I remember watching with Gert — not more than seven or eight years old, and we knew what men — I mean horses — were like. In fact, I remember being relieved when I saw Robbie for the first time, not quite a stallion thank heavens. Not a fair comparison, I know.

Poor Robbie.

I don't know why Parky called me a hussy, which she did, or a slat. I'm not. I wasn't. She had less shame than I did, often had her door partway open while she was unbuttoning herself, or in the bathroom. Her bedroom was beside mine. She used to come in without knocking all the time. I wonder what she suspected. Do You think it could have been because she —

Harriet, I say.

Where did my daughter come from? She sits straight in her chair, and her face lights up. Isn't it nice when someone's face lights up at you — I can see the little girl she was in her eyes.

Mother.

How have you been, Harriet?

Since when? she asks. Her usual concerned look is back. She's an old woman again.

I don't say anything. How am I supposed to know? Since I went away, I guess. Whenever that was.

I stare at her hands, clasped together in her lap. Old woman's hands, spotted and lined. No rings. A little gloss on the short nails, no polish.

The nurse, I tell my daughter, staring at her hands.

Do you want the nurse?

I shake my head. I don't know how to put it. I don't know how to ask for what I want. The nurse knew. The nurse knew what I wanted. I want to tell my daughter but I can't. Dammit.

She held my hand, I say.

My daughter leans over and takes my shrivelled old hand in her shrivelled old hand. She squeezes my hand gently, and strokes it. Her hands are bigger than mine, but they move lightly and delicately. It feels really nice. Thank you, I say.

She's not looking at me. She has her head up. There's noise of bells outside the room. A voice says something over the loud-speaker. More noise. Shouts and running up and down. What does it mean? I start to panic. What's wrong? I ask.

Harriet is so calm. How can she be so calm? There there, Mother, she says. She keeps stroking my hand. It's a fire drill, Mother. Don't worry.

Bells.

It's just a test, Mother. There's no danger, she says. How can she say that?

The smell of smoke hanging in the air over the harbour. The twisted blackened hull lying on its side with the water lapping against it. Crowds of people staring, crying. Ruby clutching my arm. She'd have known by then about Montgomery. First time I remember her crying. Not the last. Harriet away at university with her trunk full of clothes. Me, all in a guilty glow. Did they ever find Montgomery's body?

I've always been drawn to water; I stare into it the way other people stare into fire. I like to lose myself in the rise and fall of the warm bosom of the world. We all come from water, don't we. Ruby said once it was because I was born under Cancer, a water sign. My preoccupation with water was part of my future. I was going to die in the water, she said. It was a prevision of my own death. Ruby was full of weird shit like that — sorry, unshit. Sorry, Ruby. You know Ruby, don't You? Course You do.

Ruby was an air sign. I think that was it. She told me, smiling, that she was going to go out flying through the air. We laughed over that idea, Ruby flapping imaginary wings and crowing like a bird. That was before the fire, before she fell apart. Before I deserted her.

Her ladyship wants to see you — right now.

How to convey the venom in those words? She just spat them out at me. I was always at a loss in the face of genuine emotion. I stared at her. Yes, Miss Parker, I said, putting down my dustcloth.

She's in the little sitting room. Don't leave your cloth lying on the table, you useless girl.

Yes, Miss Parker.

The sun shone outside. I know because it made the motes I released, in dusting, dance in the light. Morning sunlight, not afternoon. I don't know what day of the week it was. Not a Thursday. I had a half-day off on Thursday.

Where are you going now? The sitting room is that way.

To the pantry, to put away my cloth, I said.

Didn't you hear me? She wants to see you right now.

Turning me around and pushing me at the stairs. She liked putting her hands on me, Parky. She was bigger than I.

Will you hold my dustcloth for me? I asked.

Do I look like a housemaid? Of course not.

The uniform had no pockets. What should I do with my cloth then? I asked.

Parker got even angrier. Can't you solve even the simplest problems for yourself, you piece of Canuck farm trash? she asked contemptuously.

Who's Canuck? I asked indignantly.

Funny to think of now, but not then. I'd never have thought of myself as anything but English. Don't ever forget that you were born in Gloucestershire, my mama told me. Canada was a stepmother, cruel and unfeeling. I lived like Snow White, dreaming of a jewelled birthright across the sea. I hung onto a mother country with all an orphan's strength. A funny thing.

Parker walked to the sitting room with me, a lot of exercise for her. She was all flushed and red in the face. Passion and a bad heart. She knocked on the door and then stood back as I entered alone. Lady Margaret didn't get up from behind the desk. Just sat there, controlled, playing with the small gold cufflink.

You sent for me, milady? I said.

And now You've sent for me. And I'm scared, and guilty, the way I was with milady.

If I were You, I'd resent all the years that Rose Rolyoke spent serving others instead of You. Serving Mama, and the Rolyokes, and Robbie, and Harriet, and all my customers.

A life of service. Sounds good, doesn't it. But I'm not good. Not really. I'm not anything, really, not right now, small and struggling with the alarms going off outside and people running.

Mama, Mama.

Above my head, swaying back and forth, the bars of the bird-cage flash. Pretty birds. Pretty pretty. And they sound so soft and quiet.

All the noise outside.

"There there," says Mama. "There there, my pretty." That's me.

And the lights go out.

A second of silence, and then everybody starts hurrying around again in the dark.

Where are the birds, I wonder. I can't see them any more.

I'm not too worried. I am a little hungry, though. I start to cry.

"There there," says Mama. Holding me tight.

The house was small and insecure, sagging between its two neighbours in the row like a tired toddler between two parents. So small it didn't have a full second storey, just a staircase up to a single room. Are you sure you wouldn't want anything grander? said the real estate agent with the big ears.

Robbie looked at me.

We have five thousand dollars, I said.

More money than I'd ever handled before, and I wasn't going to waste any of it. I'd found the bank draught in the pocket of my going-away dress. Light blue, with buttons going down the front and a high neck. I'd picked it out at Macilheeny's on Market Street in Philadelphia, on a sunny afternoon in early autumn, flies buzzing against the big west windows with their dark wood mullions. Macilheeny himself waited on us, a smirking sharp-eyed pleaser with a deep bow for Mr. Rolyoke.

Do you like it, Rose? he asked me, while Macilheeny pulled my sleeve straight.

It's beautiful, I said.

Fine, then. We'll take it.

Mr. Rolyoke drew out his wallet. Macilheeny fawned.

That morning — no, it would have been the morning before — the morning before we bought the dress I was standing in front of Lady Margaret in the small library, listening to things I didn't understand.

You'll have to go, she said.

I nodded but wondered why.

You will never see him again, she said.

Why not? Is he dead? I said, aghast.

She didn't reply. I asked again, feeling quite upset. If he was dead I wanted to know it. Has there been some kind of accident? I began.

There has been a grave miscalculation, my good slattern — and you have made it. Get out of my house this instant!

I'd have been — just — nineteen? No idea what she was talking about. I felt odd inside, had felt odd all day, wondered if maybe I was coming down with influenza. The new girl's sister was recovering from it; she'd been pretty bad, said the new girl.

Yes, milady, I said, remembering her title now that it wouldn't do me any good. Now that I didn't need it.

From behind me, a welcome voice.

Excuse me, said Mr. Rolyoke, entering the room in a cloud of pipe smoke, with a smile for me and for his wife, and a dismissive wave for Miss Parker, whom he had discovered listening outside the door.

Why can I not remember more of the night we had together? The night that made the child. A whispered greeting I recall, but the love and tenderness and leaving are gone. Next morning I woke from a dream of fulfilment with a heaviness on me, a sense of dread and unremembered loss. And it was my birthday.

What was he like? I don't know. What was Robbie like? Good and kind, fond of a laugh, and of me, not a thinker or a doer, nor yet a dreamer, which doesn't leave much, does it? He was nice and, before I married him, rich. Is that why I married him? Because he was nice? Because he was rich? Because I was pregnant and he was there? All good reasons. No. I married for no good reason. All part of the service.

Dr. Sylvester wore a concerned look. Harriet's hand was on my arm. I smiled at the doctor. How many genuinely handsome men do you meet?

Mrs. Rolyoke, are you paying attention?

Yes, doctor, I said.

Mother, are you all right?

I'm fine, I told my daughter, more harshly than I meant to. Why are we so often harsh to those who love us? Is it because we can't stand pity, or to disappoint them? Because they care too much, or not enough? I was just thinking, I told Harriet.

Yes, Mother.

She was mad at me. Maybe that's why I spoke so harshly — there's a coat of frustration underneath the caring, and frustration is a darker colour, hard to paint over.

Go on, doctor, I said. I'm listening.

He pointed his face at me but I could tell he was speaking to Harriet.

The medical tests are all negative, he said. Bloodwork, urinalysis, electrolytes — everything is normal. No diabetes or thyroid abnormality, no kidney or liver disease.

He consulted some notes here, nodding his head.

The ESR rate is negative, he went on, which means there's nothing blocking blood flow to the brain. There's no vitamin deficiency, blood and urine and CSF screens are all clean. No endocrine abnormality.

He looked up at me. I guess I'm pretty healthy then, I said.

You are a fine physical specimen, he said.

Well well. I smiled. You're not so bad yourself, I told him, but he didn't laugh. Didn't even smile. Not used to taking compliments. Harriet looked pained.

What's wrong? I said.

How long ago would this have been, now — not too long. Maybe a month. Maybe a year. These days time collapses like a folding chair. Or a road map — if you don't fold it up right you end with a pleated mess. That's the way time works for me right now.

Robbie didn't know about the bank draught. The old man likes you, he said when I showed it to him, in our Niagara Falls hotel room.

Why can't I remember Robbie better? A restless man who looked younger than he was. Kind, distracted, surprisingly good at managing Accounts Receivable. Curling ruddy hair like so many of his mother's family: I've seen photogravures of an Ainslie great aunt who looked exactly like Robbie from the neck up.

I liked the cosy house on Waverley Street, but I said no to the real estate agent. Too much, I said. He asked what we would be able to pay. I told him.

But that's a lot less, he said.

Robbie climbed up the stairs. Pretty dim it looked up there, from the sunny living room. The faint rumble of the streetcars two blocks to the north sounded like far-off thunder. From the front window I could see down to the foot of the street, where the pavement ended and the sand began. Lake Ontario, the water I'd always known, it seemed. I was ready to call this place home. Would you reconsider your first offer, ma'am? said the estate agent. I know the vendors are anxious to sell. Won't you make another offer?

Look, Rose, said Robbie, craning down from the upstairs, his face poking through the turned wooden bars of the railing. He made a face like a little child or a gargoyle, sticking out his tongue and glaring. I smiled up at him.

Just a few hundred dollars more, said the estate agent. Please, ma'am.

No, I said.

Please, Mrs. Rolyoke.

No.

A sigh from beyond the veil that falls over me now and then. I can't seem to push the veil aside, but sometimes I can hear the world through it.

If you don't eat you'll feel really sick, and we wouldn't want that.

Now there's a gap in the darkness, like a policeman with a flashlight looming out of the night. I can see my favourite nurse, the one with the tight grey hair and nobby nose, holding out a spoon full of whatever it is I'm supposed to be eating.

Oh, hello, I say.

Hello, Mrs. Rolyoke.

What is that? I ask.

Rice pudding.

She's kidding. I know what rice pudding looks like, and it isn't that. Actually, there are two kinds of rice pudding and neither one of them is that. My mama used to make rice pudding on top of the stove, thin gruel with milk and sugar and sometimes an egg for thickening. It tasted good, after cabbage — well, what wouldn't? My daddy used to go off to the barn without finishing his pudding. Mama and I would huddle together over the table to share the rest of his bowl, a spoon for me and a spoon for her. Hers was bigger than mine.

And there's another way to make rice pudding, a grand and elegant one in the oven with raisins and currants and extra eggs and cinnamon on top. Sometimes Parker made it for Mr. Davey, the chauffeur, if he'd run an errand for her. I wonder if she'd have made it for him if he hadn't run the errand. He shared with me, and I remember the feeling of wonder I had, all that cooked rich goodness. I tried to compliment Parker but she snorted and turned away.

No, I say to my nurse. I turn away my head. Just like Parky, only my face isn't red and I'm not filled with self-disgust. I like rice pudding, I say.

Then try some.

She doesn't understand. What I mean is I like rice pudding and this isn't rice pudding.

Please, she says.

I hate it when they beg. I make a no no motion with my head, back and forth, tick tock like a clock, back and forth.

Robbie loved the house. He liked the neighbourhood, with all the houses close and friendly, and the front porches with people sitting out in the cool of the summer evening. He liked the smell of the lake and the hot pavement, and summer strangers walking by with picnics and beach umbrellas. In the winter he liked the quiet, the empty cold, the walls of ice piled up around the edge of the lake. But mostly he liked to walk around the block, smoking that ridiculous pipe he never got to draw properly, maybe pushing Harriet in her pram, smiling at the people he recognized, and then come home. His face would light up when he rounded any of the corners from which he could catch a glimpse of our house. Rosie's house, he insisted on calling it. But he liked it too. Maybe he hadn't ever had anything of his own either.

Yes, the eaves hung unevenly, and the trough we put in didn't attach properly, so that in a rainstorm you could look out on a solid wall of water rolling down off the sagging roof and into the shaded climbing garden at the back.

Not much scope for flowers: a few yards of lawn in the back, even less in the front. I dug out the beds and planted — this was new for me — seeds and bulbs I'd bought. Cleaning out the basement I'd come across the book of Victorian flower language, *Love Letters from a Victorian Garden*, a thin foxed volume smelling of brickdust and rot, with a picture of motherwort on the cover. I found out that motherwort means *concealed love* — a powerful idea. I read the book over and over again, the only book in my whole life I have read more than once, surprising in myself a silent but unmistakable thrill at an instinctive understanding of a strict, arbitrary, and severely limited form of communication. Flowers are silent too, and patient, and impossible to deflect from their appointed purpose. Easy to harm but hard to kill off entirely. I sympathized with flowers. Nursing Harriet may have had something to do with my mood. Lots of time awake, with nothing to do except be there. Love. I remember thinking about love flowing out of me with my milk, filling my baby up so that she rolled over and went to sleep stuffed with love. She burped love and cried love, and threw love up all over her new nursery clock, a birthday present from Mama and Bill. Robbie, just home from work, looked pleased at the mess. He hated that clock, which chimed out the first notes of a Silly Symphony every hour. When Harriet smiled up at her daddy, standing in the nursery doorway in his last year's suit and tie, he began to chuckle.

I miss that chuckle of Robbie's. I've lived more without him than with him, but I still miss him. Whenever I think about it it makes me feel guilty. I could have loved him better.

Why are You shaking your head? What do You know about it?

Ice on my lips. Now there's a memory. Ice chips. I remember following the cart down the Dale Road to the McAllisters, who had an icebox. Wood shavings and a smell of dampness and horse. Bix was the horse's name; I can't remember the man's. He would saw a big block of ice and carry it with tongs, or else in his apron with his arms wrapped around it like a baby, a little ice baby. And when he was gone we'd — Gert and Jack and I would — steal ice chips from the cart. Well, they were going to melt anyway, weren't they?

My family didn't have an icebox. We used the back pantry as a root cellar. I remember Jack and I — wait a minute, where are these memories coming from? I haven't thought about Jack Dupree in a very long time. He was a strong healthy boy, wiry muscles and thick dark hair, shoulders that tanned to the colour of cherrywood every summer, but that would have been a lot of summers ago. Seventy-five summers ago. He's got to be dead. Not that I'm doing so much better.

Oh, Jack. The times we never had. I remember a note he sent, spring of eighth grade. *Behind the barn.* And that was all. As if there weren't thirty barns in the vicinity. But I knew which one he meant, as he knew I would. Thirteen years old, studying provinces and capitals and Christopher Columbus. And a note, slipped into an atlas — *Behind the barn*. Without a time. But I knew which time he meant, and which barn, and I guessed what he wanted to do. And do you know what? I wanted to go. I never told him. I'd like to have been able to tell him, I wanted to. To go to the barn and be with him. But I knew I couldn't. Nothing to do with being a nice girl, I just knew I couldn't. It didn't make me feel any better about it. I was still sorry. Knowledge isn't easy.

You know that, don't you? You know everything. Maybe You could try to explain it to Jack. I'm not going to get it right.

Are we going to see Dr. Sylvester again soon? I ask Harriet.

I cough. My side hurts. Harriet wipes my mouth. The bells are still ringing.

Dr. Berman is here now, she says. Don't worry, Mother.

I miss Dr. Sylvester. He's such a handsome man. Don't you think so, dear?

I know *you* do, Mother.

And his voice, I say. With that voice he could have been on radio. I loved the stories he used to tell me. Do you remember the stories he used to tell me, Harriet?

My daughter looks at me with that mixture of affection and anger that we reserve for the beloved ill. Do you really remember them, Mother?

Oh yes, I say. There was one about an airline. And another about a hockey rink. I think it was a hockey rink. And another one about a man with a pet who got lost. Or a car that broke. Something he had, and then he didn't have it. Very good stories, the way the doctor used to tell them. Do you remember them, Harriet?

She sighs, shakes her head at me. A tough time of life for her, the sixties. You don't feel old, but everyone is treating you that way, and you start to wonder if maybe they're right. I remember talking about young Jimmy Carter, and everyone laughing at me.

Who do you think is young, Harriet? I ask her. She stares at me. Doesn't understand the question. Pierre Trudeau? I ask. That Russian with the eyebrows — not Nikita Khrushchev, the other one. Oh dear. First the hockey players look young, then the policemen, then the men in the newspapers. Then it's time to pick another planet.

Mother, Dr. Sylvester wasn't telling you stories for entertainment. They were part of the memory test.

I nod my head. Yes, sometimes my memory does seem to have holes in it. Like the bucket in the song. Do you —

I remember the song, Mother.

She looks away. I've probably mentioned the song before. We used to sing it all the time. There's a hole in the bucket, dear Liza, dear Liza, there's a hole in the bucket, dear Liza, a hole. I can't remember what comes next, but the song ends the way it begins, with the hole. Like everything else I know — me too, I guess. I feel like there's a hole in my bucket, and dear Liza isn't able to do anything about it.

The bells keep ringing.

Selfish. That's what it is to be old. All you're interested in is your feelings, your pain, your memories. And how lonely you are. And what a pain the other old people are. You're sick of old people, sick of sick people, sick of sympathy. Unfortunately, you need every bit of help you can get. You can't look after yourself. Not even getting to the toilet. You're a baby again, a mewling puking whatever it is.

What are You smiling at? It's Shakespeare, isn't it? You don't have to patronize me. So I never matriculated, so what? You're as bad as Harriet, with her oboe and her anthropology. But I was so proud of her. I cried when she walked across the stage to get her handshake. You remember that. I gave everyone who came into the shop that week a free camellia japonica — *surpassing excellence*.

"Are you sure, madam?"
   "Yes, yes, quite sure."
   Mama's upset. Her hands are cold.
   "Steward, do you know — have you seen my husband?"
   "No, madam. I have not. Shall I look for him?"
   "Yes, please."
   I fret in my mama's cold hands.
   "There, there, sweetheart. Mama's here."

I never felt complete, as a mother. Nothing to do with fulfilling myself or personal achievement, I never felt whole, walking up my street with my baby in my perambulator, on my way to pick up pork chops or clothespins. There was a part of me that wasn't real, that searched and did not find. And while some of me, the outside of me, was concerned about prohibition and electric power and trade unions, and how long the Depression would last and whether Robbie would be able to keep his job in Accounts Receivable, the inside part of me wondered if I was real. What was a mother, anyway? What was a wife? A daughter? Sometimes it seemed to me that I wasn't any of these things.

෴

I went back to Cobourg once. No, twice. How could I forget? Twice. The first time we stayed at Mama's, Harriet and I. I remember her breath steaming through the scarf I wrapped around her little head. She'd have been less than a year old, born at home that spring, and she wriggled. A real handful, my stepfather called her. Bill met us at the train station in a big touring car with a big holly wreath hanging in the side window. That's right, it would have been shortly after Christmas. Cold for southern Ontario.

Mama and Bill lived in the old Daniel place on King Street, a big house with a circular carriage drive. The roof needed new slates, and the bricks needed pointing. I knew about these things because our house needed them too. It was a solid establishment, not beautiful but dignified. Mama stood on the front porch to greet us. Her breath steamed too. She had a fur wrap against the cold. She was a respectable lady now. Like me. We'd both married well.

It was an awkward visit. Robbie was in Montreal, on business, leaving right after Christmas and not due back for weeks. But that wasn't the awkward part. The awkward part was Mama. She kept, I don't know how to put it and I suppose I might have had it wrong, but it seemed to me that she was always comparing herself to me. We'd both married recently, into wealthier families. We were both living better than we ever had in our lives before. We ought to have been happy for each other. But we weren't. I wondered why.

The bells are ringing. I'm coughing. I see my daughter's face. For a second she looks like she did when she was little, and curious. Shall I tell you about when you were born? I say.

What did you say, Mother?

It was the middle of the night, I say, and your father was asleep. And suddenly something happened inside me, and I woke him up.

What?

I didn't know what was happening, I say. Neither did the doctor, exactly. But it was time for you to be born, my angel.

I can still see Robbie's face, concerned and solicitous, What's that? he kept asking. What is that on the sheets? Is that supposed to be there? Upstairs in our little room. The only upstairs room in the house.

He belonged in the house. He never belonged in the mansions in Philadelphia or Cobourg. He belonged on Waverley Street. You know how they say someone never had a chance. Too poor, too sick, too sad. Too much to cope with. Well, Robbie was rich, healthy, and happy, but he never had a chance. Until he married me, a serving girl, and ran away from his inheritance and went to work and came home to a little house with a garden, the best thing that ever happened to him, he said. This was the chance he never had.

We stared at the sheets. Disbelieving.

Call the doctor, I told him.

Are you in pain?

No, I said.

But that's blood. Is it supposed to be there?

No, I said.

Can Harriet hear me? She pushes her chair away from my bed so that she can stretch. The plastic cup full of ice chips is at her elbow. The bells are ringing. Her eyes are remote, as if she's listening to a story she's heard before, or else just bitten into a doubtful tomato.

Bill Scanlon was a good and loving man. A banker, like Uncle Brian. I wonder if Mama thought about that. He was nothing like

Uncle Brian. I sat on Bill's left at dinner, and heard what a nice day it had been, what a pleasant holiday season. They had received cards from forty-eight families, said Bill. Wasn't that a pleasing sign of respect for a newcomer like himself?

Mama asked him to pass the cruet, and he knocked over the salt cellar. Immediately, he picked up some of the spilt salt and threw it over his left shoulder. Mama sighed. That's a nice looking salt cellar, I commented, trying to make her feel better.

She sniffed. Just plated, of course, she said. I assume you have a solid silver one at home.

I smiled and couldn't think of anything to say. Thank — well, thank goodness Harriet chose this moment to set up a cry. We had her in a cradle in the small room beside the living room. The parlour, Mama called it. On my way through the door I surprised a look on her face: fierce, angry, envious. I felt uncomfortable. I knew who she was upset with, and why.

Of course it was me. But not because I had married Philadelphia old money. Not because my father-in-law controlled a troubled commercial empire, at least that's how the newspapers put it. She hated me because of Harriet. Because I had a baby and she didn't.

Dr. Wilson lived around the corner. His children were always offering to mow our lawn or shovel our walk. I heard his voice in the downstairs hall, comforting Robbie, who sounded hysterical. Put some water on to boil, the doctor said. There's a good chap. We'll all have a cup of tea. He wore a shirt and pants over his pyjamas. He smiled down at me in a friendly way, asked how I was.

Is the baby coming? I asked. It isn't supposed to be for another two weeks; you told me, doctor.

Maybe I was wrong. It happens, you know, he said.

There wasn't very much blood. I asked if that was good.

I don't know, he said.

And I don't seem to be in pain. Not at all, I said.

He nodded, went away for a moment to wash his hands.

Well, not too much pain, I said when he got back.

His thinning dark hair was tousled and stiff with yesterday's pomade. He needed a shave. He had a bulbous nose and glasses. His hands were warm.

But I didn't come out yet, Harriet would say, looking up from her bowl of soup. This conversation would have happened around the dinner table, just the two of us while Robbie was in the North Atlantic, winning the war. That's what the newspapers said.

No, you didn't come out right away, I'd say. With a grimace of remembrance. Not yet.

Robbie showed us pictures of the HMCS *Stadacona*, his first leave. Isn't she a beauty, he said. Clean lines, narrow entry, turns practically in her own length. I could hardly look. So scared. Twenty-five knots top speed, he told me, 2800 tons displacement. Wow, said Harriet, peering. In the picture the seas were taller than the ship, heavy with menace. Where are you, Father? she asked. Somewhere under all that flying water, he said with a laugh.

Nineteen forty. It was like having a stranger in the house, a man I'd never seen before and wouldn't see again. Not an adventure, though. And not romantic. I've never been more scared.

Was I waiting for him to die? Is that it? Or was I waiting for him to turn into Daddy?

He didn't of course. Never got the chance to. But he wouldn't have, I'm pretty sure. He was more alive in the war, not less. He talked about it when he was home, which wasn't often — a week at a time, after three or four convoys in a row.

I'm scared all the time, he told me, walking in the park in the spring, smell of dog and new growth, Harriet at school. We're all scared, from the captain on down. But we have a job to do, and the job becomes more important than how you're feeling. Do you understand?

I said I did.

During Action Stations I run aft to my post as fast as I can, check all the depth charges, assign the men their duties, and report to the lieutenant on the bridge. And then I wait. And the time passes in waiting. The waiting becomes the job. I'm scared, and so are the men, but even waiting is more important than being scared. I don't like them telling jokes, because jokes make the waiting easier. I don't want the time to go faster. I want to do a better job.

So intense, so serious. With his cap pulled down and the cigarette in the corner of his mouth, he looked just like a recruiting poster. My Robbie. He knew what he was. He knew what he had to do. I understood the pull of a uniform. Girls like a man with confidence. I reached my arm around him and gave him a hug. He looked down, startled. Not used to this kind of display from me. Then he put his arm around me, and we walked on, arm in arm, alone in our own fears.

Not afraid of fire, or being buried alive. Not afraid of accident or sickness, or falling from a height. Not afraid of bullets, not even after last year. Maybe a bit. I'd never seen a pistol before. So disappointing and small. And the poor youngster holding it, shaking in his shaking hand, a baby really, for all the terrible language, I could tell by the need in his face. And the tears that came when I said, Oh you poor thing. Anticlimax, both the weapon and the wielder, except that they can kill you.

Not afraid of ropes or dark places, or snakes. Not afraid of blindness or going crazy — which is probably just as well.

Not afraid of anger. Lady Margaret Rolyoke stood in the doorway of the ugly summer mansion I knew so well, a bubbling cauldron of hurt and disappointment and rage. She didn't speak to me, of course. Why did you come? she demanded of her son.

This was my other visit back to Cobourg, a warm day in early summer. A new servant at the screen door behind Lady Margaret, pretty, gaping at us. I knew the face but not her name. She recognized me all right. Everyone knew me, I discovered when I got off the train. I was the local girl who ran off with the Rolyoke boy. The station master's son called me ma'am, which pleased and shocked me. He was my age.

A horse and cart waiting behind us, with enough luggage to last a few nights. Light rain falling from a sky of pewter. A crying baby, a standing horse, a best dress which I could get into again, now that the baby was a year old. All these imperatives.

The familiar grounds looked beautiful. The flower beds were well forward — hard work by Adam. I couldn't help noticing daffodil and elder blossom — *compassion* and *regard*, supposedly.

Harriet wiggling. Robbie standing still. A look in his eyes I didn't recognize at the time, but remembered later. Tense, troubled, decisive. Robbie saying, I thought you'd like to see your granddaughter. She can walk now.

Lady Margaret not looking. Not looking at the baby I held in my arms. Not looking in my direction. Staring at her son with eyes of flint. That woman cannot come into my house, she said and then, turning finally to face me, *You* — virulent harpy, spitting with the force of her words, cheeks mottled like a rare seashell, pointing her finger with deadlier intent than the poor mugger did his pistol — *you cannot come into my house.*

Back to her son. That woman — me, you understand — is evil! she said, sounding like Jimmy Sunday. She cannot enter here.

Robbie's face slammed shut like a door in a gale, but he didn't move for a long time, while the servant looked on in horrified fascination. It takes a while to say goodbye, doesn't it. At least I assume that's what Robbie would have been doing — saying goodbye.

I didn't know what he felt. Back in the cart, his face was slack and shut. I suppose he'd thought the grandchild would change his mother's feelings. Are they expecting us? I'd asked, before we left. He strapped up a suitcase and told me not to worry.

I didn't know what he felt now. You want to know someone, to understand what drives them, what they're worried about, where they go when they go away. Easy enough with the mugger, what was his name again, Jack, Joe, something like that. Not Jack. It seems a long time ago, for all it was just last week — last year, I mean. Robbie has been dead for over half a century and yet it's like he just died yesterday.

Joe, the mugger, was in pain. All the time, in the shock of a criminal action, in the tension of the moment, inside himself, pain. I saw it clear as television. Maybe because I was an older woman, and in pain myself.

You poor thing, I told him, and he curled up like a flower at sunset. His gun drooped. I can't give you any money, I told him, I don't have any. Sorry, I said. Behind him the coloured lights flashing from the corner store, and the traffic passing, and the empty night.

I thought of Ruby, all the things I hadn't done for her.

I live near here, I said. Would you like to come up for a cup of tea?

I'm sorry, I told Robbie. I'm sorry about your mother.

He nodded.

I wonder where your dad is? I asked.

He looked at me, and his eyes were empty. As if he wasn't there at all. What'll we do now, Rosie? he asked. A little boy who realizes that running away from home means not coming back. Where'll we go? he asked.

I asked the cart driver to take us to the Arlington Hotel.

We rolled away with a jerk, and Robbie, sitting beside me, put his arm around my shoulders. His face, under the empty eyes, was a smiling mask. I wonder what mine looked like.

Does it hurt to have babies? I can't tell you the number of times Harriet asked that. So interested, who could have foreseen she'd never have any? All right, who else? I wonder if she wanted them? I wonder if she tried to have one, and couldn't? What are You frowning for? I'm her mother, don't I ... no, I suppose not. None of my business. I hate the word *barren*, though. So technical — makes a woman a piece of geography.

You're still frowning. Why?

Well, look at Harriet, brought up with soup on the table and roller skates on her feet. Brought up with school for as long as she wanted. I would have given so much to be able to go to school until I was twenty-two. By the time she graduated I'd been working hard for I couldn't say how long. And what had she done? Found out about Samoan aboriginals, and Arcturus, and played one of Beethoven's symphonies in a concert filled with proud parents.

I'm sorry. I know I sound petty. It's just that so much of my life seems to have been taken up with service to an unknown end.

Did Robbie love me? Did he? He seemed to. He said he did. But did he? There's no one I can ask, nothing I can point to to say, yes, he did.

I don't even know if I loved him.

I don't understand, Dr. Wilson muttered.

What, is it? Is there a problem? I panted between contractions.

No problem. None at all. The doctor smiled at me.

Is the baby going to be all right? I asked.

Sure, the baby will be fine when he comes out. Or she. The doctor took a sip of cold tea.

Robbie came in again. He'd been coming and going for a while. I don't like it, he said. She should be in the hospital.

Dr. Wilson looked embarrassed. Sorry, my boy, he said.

The doctor had privileges, that's what he called them, at the General Hospital, and I should have been there, but Toronto was in the middle of an influenza outbreak, and there were no spare beds. Dr. Wilson offered to get me to another hospital, but he warned that he would not be able to attend the birth there. And it'll be more expensive, he added. Robbie choked, said it didn't matter, we'd pay anything to keep me out of danger.

Didn't he say that? It would have been like him. It's the way I remember it.

Dr. Wilson laughed and said I wasn't in danger, and that if I went to hospital I'd probably end up catching influenza myself. Nasty places, hospitals, he said. Full of sick people, you know. My advice to all my patients is to stay healthy, he said. Stay away from hospitals.

And so I was born at home, Harriet would say with a sparkle in her eye, on a blustery spring morning, to save a fifty-dollar fee.

Now now, I'd say.

And I was a beautiful baby.

That you were, I'd say.

And bald.

Yes. A bright bouncing baby girl, with eyes the colour of a star-filled twilight, and dimples in your head from the doctor's fingertips.

And my father was there.

He was, I'd say. Well, in the next room, drinking tea and smoking, and calling out every few minutes to ask if it was over.

I'm glad, Harriet would say, that I was born.

So am I.

Am I bleeding again? I asked the doctor, when it was all over.

No. He smiled down at me and the baby. The cleanest birth I've ever been at. You both did a marvellous job.

She was asleep on my stomach, little unnamed girl.

Then what was the bleeding before? I asked with a yawn.

If I didn't know any better, Dr. Wilson began.

Hmmm?

Well, when I was examining you, to see if you were dilated....

My eyes were closing. I tried to pay attention.

It was just a membrane, he said.

Membranes bleed? I wondered.

Oh yes, he said. When they're broken. Rest now.

Hearing that we were in town, at the hotel — and news like that travels at the speed of sound — Mama invited us to dinner. She would have invited us to stay, she told me, but Bill's brothers were visiting from the east coast.

Robbie sat beside Mama, who was nervous and hyperexcited to be entertaining one of Cobourg's famous imports in her own house. The rich Americans spent their summers in a kind of forbidden city, partying and dining among themselves, seldom venturing downtown, never attending local functions. And here was the scion of a rich Yankee family, one of the Cobourg four hundred — though actually I suppose there would have been about forty, don't You think? Forty Families of Distinction — at her own dining table. She felt proud and inadequate, socially fulfilled and yet filled with doubt.

Robbie was nervous, distracted by the memory of his own mother's anger, eager to please but unsure of what was expected of him. Of course, Mama kept saying, Philadelphia is more metropolitan than Cobourg. How happy we were to see you and your father there, at the wedding.

Robbie smiled mechanically, nodded, ate his meat with every appearance of enjoyment.

Of course this lamb is local — and yet I wonder if you can boast of such tenderness in Philadelphia high society, she said.

Robbie reminded her that we lived in Toronto now. But I do remember, he admitted, that the spring lamb we used to eat in Rittenhouse Square was not as fresh as what we got in Cobourg in the summer.

It was odd to hear him call Mama Mrs. Scanlon.

There, you see, dear. Mama flashed a wide smile down the table at me. I tried to return it. I was talking to one of Bill's brothers. I can't remember which. There were three brothers, and they had the habit of referring to each other by Christian name and nickname interchangeably. It was difficult to keep track of Moe and Peter and, was it Arthur? And Dog Face and Flat Top and, what was the other one, The Gord. Actually, poor Dog Face was easy to remember because he looked it. And he didn't mind. Call me Dog Face, he told me, when I stumbled.

They called my stepfather Red. Of course by now he wasn't Red any more, he was grey. But no one gets a nickname late in life. One moment on the playground you're Frank, or whatever, and the next you're Dog Face, and that's it. Goodbye Board of Directors. Goodbye politics. No one's going to elect Senator Dog Face, or Premier Dog Face. Even Commissioner Dog Face is going to be an uphill battle. Get into business for yourself, or move out of town as soon as you can. Live among strangers and start over.

So there we were around a hastily improvised festive board, Mama and Robbie and me, and the variously named brothers Scanlon. I felt like I was in the middle of a Russian novel — which is farther than I've ever got.

Bill was the youngest in his family, the only one who'd gone to university, gone into a profession instead of the family business, left the Maritimes. His brothers made all sorts of jokes about him, but there was affection too. They liked visiting the black sheep. Imagine baby Red having a granddaughter, they said, laughing heartily. Bill didn't seem to mind. Looking back at Bill, dead I don't know how long now, I don't think he ever minded anything. His first words to me at my mother's funeral were, How nice to see you, Rose. Isn't it a lovely day? It's not that he was oblivious, like poor Daddy, preoccupied with an insupportable evil. More stoic, determined to appreciate the present and bear the past without comment. Blind to complication, maybe, wearing glasses that filtered out the subtle shades of life. My mother looked queenly, slow moving and studied, ordering dessert as if she was opening parliament. The servant — yes, she had a servant, Bill said she shouldn't have to be doing any heavy work at her time of life, and anyway they could afford it — was a local girl I remembered from years before. I tried to strike up a conversation with her but she got all reserved and shy.

They're very good to me here, she said, very fast, head bent down to the floor. I get all I want to eat, can even take home some to my family.

How is the family, Janet? I asked. She had a brother and sister, a mother who worked hard and a dad who didn't.

They're fine, um, she said, unable to think what to call me.

All three of the visiting brothers — they were something to do with importing and exporting, had done very well at it until recently, nothing moving into or out of Halifax without them taking a cut, though trade was so slow these days — were nice to me. And why not? I was young and pretty, and it was spring. When

Harriet started to cry, one of them — Arthur or Moe, I can't remember which one — came along. Kootchie kootchie, he called to the baby, tickling her under her chin. Harriet stopped crying and pulled his finger back and forth. Moe — I think that's who it was — looked pleased.

She's so tiny, he said.

So tiny. The hand in front of me is so tiny. Pale pink crescents, tiny wrinkles, soft smooth skin, dimpled at the knuckles. Whose is it? Is it mine? Can this waving amorphous thing, this palely floating blob of movement and feeling, can this be me too?

"Come on," says the voice from the dazzling above. "Come on."

"No," says Mama.

And the sound of water, rushing.

Robbie was feeling more wakeful than I that night. Old Dog Face is an interesting fellow, he told me, as we were getting ready for bed.

I didn't say anything.

You know, the Scanlons have done well for themselves. Dog Face and his brothers pretty much control the warehousing in the eastern provinces, he said.

Harriet was in a little crib beside the bed. She was still sleeping. Such tiny hands.

The hotel room was small. Robbie's eyes followed me as I got undressed.

How are you feeling, Rose? he asked.

I was tired, and a little irritable. I don't apologize for it; I'll bet Your mother was irritable when You were being weaned. Wasn't she? Come on now.

Twin beds in the room. Robbie in a nightshirt, sitting on my bed. His bed untouched. Lights out but it was as bright as morning inside, thanks to the new electric streetlighting outside the window.

You know, Rose, he said. I was talking to Dr. Wilson.

What about Dr. Wilson? I asked.

Robbie looked embarrassed. Well, the doctor said that we've been ... that you and I have been doing ...

And he stopped. What have we been doing? I asked. Harriet would be hungry in a couple of hours and I wanted to get some sleep.

No, wait. That would have been later, wouldn't it? When we wanted another child, and we tried and couldn't and Robbie went to the doctor, and he said —

A lot later.

That night in the Arlington Hotel Robbie looked so sweet and excited that my bad mood broke like a soap bubble, and I smiled and pulled him into my bed. His large, white hands were trembling, and there was tobacco on his breath, and sherry from the trifle we'd had for dessert. He was so gentle — but then he always was.

When Harriet woke up and cried, he didn't move for a minute. Tastes funny, he said, sitting up. I pushed him away.

Bright lights in a dark bedroom. I remember a night with the moon low on the horizon, the shape and colour of a snowball. Nice idea, a snowball, the night was so hot I could feel sweat rolling off me. I stood at my window, staring out at the moon, and the barn, and the hard earth, and the failing crop. I heard a kitchen chair fall over as my daddy stood up. I heard a mosquito in my ear, brushed it away angrily. I was listening for silence. The springs in the mattress next door creaked and complained to each other as he lay down. A minute later he began slowly, powerfully, regularly, to snore. I relaxed, and hopped up onto my windowsill, and whispered into the fertile summer silence. I love you, I whispered. I love you I love you I love you so much.

I love you too, Rose, he said. No, that wasn't it.

You're too good to me, Rose, he said.

No, I'm not.

Do you mind if I call you Rose? I think he asked in his quiet, educated voice. Sometimes he sounded like a radio announcer, and sometimes like the teacher at Precious Corners' School, only with a hint of an accent because of course he was from abroad.

Of course not. I call you David, don't I? Let me look after you, Lieutenant David Godwin. You're wounded, aren't you? Here, lean on me, I said.

My arm held out to the warm and empty air, I walked slowly across the bare boards to my lonely bed, supporting my invisible beloved.

I'm burning up. That's what it feels like. So hot. So dry. My eyes flutter open and shut, and all I see is a desert of light. I'm lying down. Figures hovering over me, like vultures. Go away, I say. Love is a vanished dream, a memory of nothing. Poor Jack, the lover I never had. And poor David, the lover that never was.

The vultures are weeping. Not the way they look on the nature shows. I'm thirsty.

Here, Mother.

I open my eyes. Harriet holds out a glass of water. Her hand is trembling. Poor Harriet — she isn't as young as she once was. I take the water.

How is the binding going? I ask her.

She frowns. Mother?

You know — oh I've forgotten the word again — the thing you do. How's the Bluestone case going? I asked.

What about the Bluestone case?

How's it going? I ask.

Mother, the Bluestone case was a long time ago.

I'm thirsty, I say.

She gestures. Then drink your water.

Thank you.

She smiles at me. How can she smile at me? I'm a stupid and forgetful old woman. Clumsy too. Sorry, I say, wiping myself with my free hand.

That's okay, Mother.

Yes it is, isn't it? We smile at each other. We've fallen out of the habit, but it's easy to pick up again.

Investigating, I say. That's the word I was trying to remember. Investigating.

Her face clouds over. Is she thinking back to the Bluestone case? Reporting on it, one of the magazines called her a miracle worker.

I used to be an investigator, Mother, she says calmly. I gave it up — remember?

Yes of course, I say.

Dog Face! I cried, loud enough for everyone in the hotel lobby to hear. He blushed. Flat Top! The Gord! What are these? I asked.

They smiled and held out their hands, like three swells inviting the same chorus girl to dinner. But the presents weren't for me.

Happy birthday to you, they sang together, happy birthday to you, happy birthday dear Harriet — lingering over the word, eyes down at the pram — happy birthday to you.

Robbie came back from the booking office with our train tickets.

He shook hands with the Scanlon brothers. You shouldn't have, fellows, he said.

She already had her birthday. Weeks and weeks ago, I said.

The Silly Symphony clock from Mama and Bill had arrived right on the day.

So we're a bit late, said Dog Face. She won't care.

I lifted Harriet out of the pram to say thank you to her sort-of uncles, and she got three kisses and started to cry.

We opened the gifts at home. There was a wooden ship, and a pillow with a picture of King George embroidered on it. We kept them for a long time. Harriet used to take down the ship when Robbie was away at sea, fighting. I can't remember the third present.

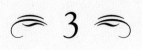

Presentation

I was so proud of Harriet, marching away from me in her hat and cape. So grown up she looked, so mature. Hard to believe she was just a little girl. Bye, Mother, she said. Over her shoulder, tugging herself away from my restraining hand, eager to be off and playing with her friends before the bell rang. Bye, Harriet. Play carefully. You know, she's always been well-behaved, I told her teacher. So polite and gentle. I tried to teach her how to be a real lady.

Her teacher was a girl, just out of school herself, with an overbite. No, it was a bald man in a gown. I wonder what the little kids made of him. Your daughter is a hard worker, Mrs. Rolyoke, he said. You must be so proud of her.

Oh, I am. I am. She's so grown up.

Cake and coffee on a lawn, with cannons and bells, noisy things when they went off — not the cannons. The bells were going off though, from the clock tower. Oh God Our Help in Ages Past. I wondered what time that made it.

I understand she wants to be a lawyer. Is that right?

I nodded and bit into my cake. A lawyer. When she was a little girl, she and I played school at home, I told the bald man. I was never a very good student. She used to threaten me with the strap.

Now that's odd, isn't it? She did used to threaten me, funny plain little girl she was, with her flashing eyes. And her hand poised in the air. I would pretend to cower and promise to do my work better next time, and she would let me off. That was her, wasn't it? Not Parker, with a wooden spoon in her hand. Funny the way the pictures blur. I can still feel the bite of that spoon on my rear end. Parky used to like to hit me there. Not just me, the other girls too. The pretty ones. I suppose it was the most obvious spot. Bend over the table, she'd say in her grating voice. And I — well, at least once I said no.

Robbie was proud of her too — look at my great big girl, he would say, coming home from Accounts Receivable to hear all about kindergarten. What pretty numbers you write, so neat, he would say. She probably got it from him; I was never a neat writer. But Harriet always put things in rows. I was so proud of her. And so was — funny, I was going to say Robbie but he was dead by then — so was Geoff.

You must be Harriet's father, said the bald man in the gown. Sipping his tea, looking over our shoulders. And Geoff smiled and shook his head. Just a family friend, he said.

What a friend. He'd driven me all the way to Kingston, more than three hours, just because I asked. And he looked good in a conservatively tailored dark suit. A little hairy, but presentable.

That's eglantine, isn't it, I said, pointing at the border of the garden. The man in the gown didn't know. Very appropriate to graduation exercises, I told him. It signifies genius and poetry. A pretty colour too, I said. I walked closer to examine it. Geoff took a bite of his sandwich. The man in the gown turned away to talk to someone else's parents. The bells started to play one of the Silly Symphonies.

No, I said, no no no.

And Harriet giggled and put down her hand. What is nine times twelve? she asked in her high but stern voice. Would either of us have known? I don't think so. You are a funny mother, she said. And then the stairs fell down.

We were safe of course, safe in the bedroom turned schoolroom on the second floor. At the top of the stairwell we peered down, on our stomachs, as the dust rose in the hole that had been our staircase.

Harriet giggled. Eight years old and safe with her mom. I smelled dusty summer foliage, saw a ladder twisted on the ground. Don't worry, I said. Your father will get us down.

Who's worried? Now, Mother, what is the capital of Asia?

I don't know, I said.

I heard the sound from Parky's room, muffled but regular, knocked and opened the door because I'd read a story in a magazine about a man in despair hanging himself and all they could hear was his heels pounding on the wall and then the sound disappeared and they found him and it was too late.

No no no, I said, and Parky looked up. It wasn't me she was spanking this time, but a new girl, pretty as a doll, fine bones and features, and fragile. I'm surprised she could get a job in service. She looked sick and beautiful, not long for this world.

You know her. You must see her kind in droves.

Don't tell, she said. Please don't tell.

Parker was swearing to herself, wouldn't look at me, her face as red as amaryllis, *timid* and *proud*. Hands clenching and opening like the muscles of her heart.

Don't tell, the new girl whispered again, pulling down her petticoat, or I'll lose my place.

She broke off, covered her mouth and coughed, hard. Poor thing.

Oh, I said. And left.

Well, what would You have done?

Through the rising dust I could just see the front hall. The telephone was in the kitchen. There was nothing to do but wait. Harriet and I tried pounding on the walls like the hanging man in the story. We shared one bedroom wall with the house south of us. Number 115 Waverley, two widows and a cat.

No one answered. I didn't even know if they were home. Mother, look. There's our living room. Doesn't it look funny from up here?

Yes it does, I said. Cut off from the world with nothing but a bed and a portable blackboard, I felt neither hunger nor thirst, nor the panic of an animal in a trap. I was safe. My daughter was safe. I leaned over, put my arms around her, and hugged her hard.

The phone rang in the kitchen.

You want to stare down the hole some more, I asked, or do you want to play school?

Harriet crawled back up onto her knees. School, she said. The phone kept ringing.

Hanging up, I could still hear Robbie's voice inside my ear, like a train away in the distance. Then Harriet came home from school, letting the screen door bang. Look, Mother! she cried, dropping her satchel and sweater, showing off a small black box with metal clasps.

Harriet, dear, you must —

No, look!

Surprising complexity inside the box, black and silver nestled in blue velvet. Machinery or jewellery, it was hard to say.

It's an oboe, Mother. The music teacher chose me to play it. Me!

Her first term at Royal Park Collegiate. My little girl was growing up fast. Not many friends yet, but she'd never been much of a mixer. No boys, of course. If only she had let me do something with her hair, but she was always busy, and she didn't mind what she looked like. She worked so hard. So hard.

See Mother, you put it together like this. And you stick the reed in the end. See?

I nodded, not really paying attention.

And then you blow like this. I mean, like this.

Fingers clamped down, cheeks puffed out, she looked ridiculous. No sound came out. The end of the instrument quivered like a — like something. She took the reed out of her mouth to gasp for air.

Your father just called from Halifax, I said. He's got a week's leave. He'll be home tomorrow.

Hurray! Then she gasped some more. Will he be home for dinner? she asked.

I think so, I said.

Can we have macaroni and cheese?

I think so.

Good.

Her cheeks puffed again.

Is Harriet's father here? asked another tea-drinking professor, a younger man than the last one, in an older gown.

Harriet's father — that is, my husband was killed. During the war, I said.

Funny way to put it: during the war, rather than in the war. Made Robbie seem like a conscientious objector or something. He was in the navy, I said.

The young man in the gown frowned sympathetically. How brave of you, he said.

Me? I choked on a sip of tea. Brave of me?

He took my hand. Alone, in wartime, he said. Just you and your daughter. Both of you wondering where your husband was. Wondering how he died.

Oh, we knew that, I said. We buried him out of the home.

Mother? Mother? Harriet running up. She ran smoothly, good wind — maybe from all that oboe playing. Not like me. I used to run with a curious knock-kneed grace, melting hearts and losing footraces. I can't run at all now, of course, with my broadloom. Damn it, what is it called? It aches like a train going up and down your leg. Mother? called Harriet.

I open my eyes. Are you still here? I say. She doesn't say anything. Or is this another visit? I say. I can't remember her saying goodbye.

Are you all right, Mother? You were moaning.

The pain in my leg, I say.

What was that? she says. She can't hear me.

The pain, I say.

Poor Mother.

Harriet has a scarf on her head. She didn't have a scarf last time, did she? Maybe it's another visit.

And your father, I say. I was remembering the time the staircase came down and we were stranded at the top. And your father rescued us with a ladder from the house next door with the two widow ladies.

She isn't paying attention.

I try to swallow and can't. My throat sucks together like the inside of a bag with no air. I fumble for a drink. Harriet holds it for me, and I sip. Actually, I don't. I don't seem to get anything at all. But I feel wet. I look down.

Oh, Mother, she says.

I'm wet down my front. Isn't that drinking, when you do that with your mouth? Damn it all, you'd think a skill like drinking would be there whenever you wanted it.

Sorry, I say. She brings the drink back. Concentrate, concentrate. Got it. That's not bad. A word drifts across my memory, like the clouds that used to drift past my apartment window. Orange.

Good for you, she says, taking my glass. Then she says something else.

I beg your pardon, I say.

She bends down. Don't worry, she says. They'll come for us soon.

She's very close to me. I can smell orange on her breath too. The bells are loud, she says. Aren't they?

You can hear them? I say.

Of course, she says. Can't you?

That's a relief, I say.

She sits up.

There aren't always bells. This must be the same visit.

Will you be going soon? I ask.

What? Sorry, Mother, I can't hear.

I repeat my question. I speak slowly and loudly, so she will understand.

A bran muffin, she says. And juice. You had some Jell-O.

I lie back against the propped pillows.

I was talking to Dr. Wilson today, said Robbie.

Oh yes?

Odd topic to bring up, I thought, and an odd time too. Ten o'clock at night, the two of us lying on my bed in the dark. Oh yes? I said.

I talked about us wanting to have a child. Another one, I mean. The doctor was very understanding. He talked about cycles — that is, uh, your cycles.

I didn't say anything.

And then the doctor said a lot of couples have this problem, but we had one child, and we were just to keep trying. And I made a joke — you know, about ...

His voice trailed off. I looked down towards the bottom of the bed. My bare knee was very white, almost ghostlike, against the dark-coloured cotton of my nightdress. I turned my head and peered down at my other knee. It looked ghostlike too, only the nightdress was hiked farther up on that side. Robbie's face inches from mine. His body on mine, between my outspread knees. He peered down at me. Are you okay, Rose? Am I hurting you?

Oh no, I said.

When I was leaving the doctor's I made a joke about ... well, about this, what we're doing, said Robbie, moving against me. The bed groaned, and my nightdress rode up a little more.

He stopped moving. His face inches from mine.

We're doing it wrong, Rose, he said.

The automatic doors of Warden Grace Villa opened slowly. The lobby was bright, with lots of windows and a white floor with little coloured chips in the smooth stone. Everyone seemed to be in a wheelchair. I felt athletic, leaning on my walker.

The door swished shut behind me, leaving me in a pleasantly warm atmosphere, a nice change. Lots of places were making me cold. I smiled at the man nearest me. Staring at nothing through the thickest lenses I've ever seen. With lenses like that a normal person would be able to see Pluto, or angels dancing. An old man in a cardigan and slippers. Hello, there, I said, giving him my very best smile. He ignored me. Maybe I wasn't far enough away.

Come on, Mother, said Harriet.

I'm coming, dear, I said.

My room — the first room I had — was painted green. The curtains were filmy. They fluttered in the draft from the heat vent. I watched them fluttering all night long, and in the morning Dr. Sylvester had forgotten my name.

Mrs. — he said, and then stopped, his fresh smiling face momentarily clouded by an unusual doubt. Well, I know how he felt. I'm like that all the time. How are you, he said, sincerely. He was really interested.

The nurse with him was the evil one — black hair and marks all over her face. She held a fresh yellow folder with me inside it.

She was crying, said the nurse. All through the night.

I'm so sorry, said the doctor, and he meant it. Didn't he? The folder was in his hand now, and he looked at it for a moment and called me by name. Rose, he said, sitting beside me, taking my hand in his. Cold hands they were, I remember.

Where's my daughter? I said.

You mustn't cry, Rose. You're here for a while, you might as well get used to it. Joan here wants you to be happy. She's your friend.

I wondered what he meant by a while.

Will I go home, I asked, and then forgot the word for the day after this day. Will I go home ... Wednesday?

The doctor stood up with a long flowing movement, and the curtains followed him, swirling. Behind them the sun was bright and there were those mare's-tail clouds swishing across the sky. Oh, Robbie, I thought, as I always do when I see them. Take warning, my dear. Which didn't make much sense in 1941, when he was a thousand miles away from me, and even less sense now that he was dead.

Who sleeps there? I asked, pointing across the room.

No one, just yet. Someone new will be coming in tomorrow, said Joan. Smiling at the doctor. Then at me. Just think, you'll have a roommate, dear.

They think you're blind.

Then whose slippers are those? I asked. Pointing at the floor under the other bed.

Joan picked them up hurriedly.

Would you like something to drink? asked Dr. Sylvester.

Then I heard the announcement. *Good morning. Today is Thursday, June the seventh,* a pause, and the voice continued, *1997. Exercise classes begin in ten minutes in the lounge.*

Mornings were the worst. Cold and tired from the night, with a day to get through before I could be cold and tired again. Daddy snoring in the other bedroom, Uncle Brian snoring on the daybed. I haven't thought about that daybed in a long time. It was a nightbed too. My uncle lived with us for years and never had a proper place to sleep. I wonder where he put his clothes. And Mama and I tiptoeing around, careful not to wake the men, lighting the stove, shivering while the wood caught, coughing into our sleeves. I seemed always to have a dripping nose and soiled handkerchiefs. Usually I would get out of the house before Daddy woke up, groaning and retching and moving slowly through the kitchen, waiting for Mama to find him a bowl to throw up in. He never shivered; I don't know if he even felt the cold. His feet would be bare, sometimes, the toenails thick and yellow and curling. Gert's house was only a mile away. They had hot water. By the time the two of us left for school I would be feeling cleaner.

I don't open my eyes. They're open all the time. But I see Harriet now. Hello, I say.

Mother, how are you feeling?

Mornings are the worst, I say. She smiles that smile that says I've got it wrong again. I guess it isn't morning. Not that I give a shit.

Where were you that night? I ask.

Which night, Mother?

When I first came to this land. I mean this place. Warden Grace Villa. I cried all night long. When I first came to this land — that's a song, isn't it. When I ... damn.

There there, Mother.

I close my mouth. Didn't realize I was talking out loud. So much of my life seems to take place inside my head these days. I must have really said the words then, instead of just thinking them. Sorry. Unshit. Undamn.

I was all alone, I say, in a strange place with a dead person. No wonder I was crying.

Mother?

The doctor was nice, but he didn't come until the next morning. All night by myself, left like an old drunk at the luggage office.

There there, Mother.

I mean trunk, I say. Not drunk.

Yes, Mother dear.

You don't know what I'm talking about do you?

Yes, Mother. That's right.

Poor Harriet.

Hey, I want some roses, she said. I'd seen her around the neighbourhood.

What colour? I asked.

Red — what other colours are there?

Some people are so ignorant. This was a grown woman, just about my height, well dressed, long hair wound uncomfortably around her head, with a little hat perched on top.

I was just starting out in the business, so I started to explain. The difference between full red and deep red and burgundy, between buds and blooms and pink and yellow and Marechal niel and Montiflora. She listened hard. Her face was a good one for listening, didn't move around much. Little pointed chin and hard eyes.

Which one would you pick as a gift for me? she said.

For you? A musk rose, I said, without hesitating. See? I showed her some. In the language of flowers, a musk rose signifies *capricious beauty*, I said. Her little closed face opened wide suddenly, and she laughed out loud. I found myself smiling. I'd been open a week and hadn't had a lot of smiles.

Capricious beauty? I'll take a dozen, she said. Hey, do you smoke?

She offered a pack. I shook my head. She lit one, stared around the store.

How long you been open? Not long, right?

I nodded. Her eyes narrowed suspiciously.

How many different kinds of rose you got?

I answered truthfully. Two kinds, I said.

Capricious Beauty and what else?

I'm the other — my name is Rose, I said.

She laughed and laughed. And stuck out her hand.

I'm Ruby. She blew smoke at me, laughing.

Robbie hardly drank at all. He'd shake his head when I offered him some more wine at dinner. I nearly fell off my park bench when he slid down beside me and said, Let's go for a drink.

I have never known much about the places I've lived. I hardly knew Cobourg at all, even though I lived right outside it. The only part of Toronto I ever knew was the eastern Beaches, where our house was, and my store. And, much later, my apartment. I heard about other parts of the city: Rosedale, Sunnyside, Hogg's Hollow. They weren't too far away — a tram ride or two, an hour or two — but I never visited. They might as well have been movie places, Babylon or Shangri-La. I remember frowning into the darkness of the movie theatre, watching Cary Grant and Katharine Hepburn in Philadelphia. I'd been there too — in fact I'd worked in a house a lot like the one in the movie, only downtown instead of out in the country. But I didn't know the city well. I lived there for two winters and I don't think I ever went farther north than New Street, where the butcher Lady Margaret used — the one whose lamb wasn't as good as Cobourg's — had his shop. On my half-day off I walked to the Independence Hall bus depot, paid a nickel to ride the Number 4 tram to Harbor Park. I watched the boats, then rode the bus back. I didn't expect to see anyone I knew, and I never did. Not until Robbie, anyway.

What? I said. Oh, hello, sir.

A drink, Rose. Come on, it's your day off. And you can call me Robbie.

I nearly fell off the bench, I tell You.

Five nines are forty-five. Six nines are fifty-six. No, they aren't, but damned if I know what they are right now. Mind you, I didn't know what they were then.

Mother?

There are strange things done 'neath the midnight sun by the men who moil for gold, I say. The Arctic trails have their secret tales that ... that would make fifty-four.

Oh, dear, she says. Poor Mother.

I used to know that. We all had to recite it in school. Did you have to learn the poem, Harriet? I ask. There are strange things done 'neath the midnight sun by the men who —

Mother? Are you feeling all right?

I struggle up to a sitting position. Of course I'm all right, I say. Seven nines are sixty-three. Eight nines are ... I feel pretty good, I say. Mind you, you look kind of tired, Harriet. Should you take a nap or something?

A very grey afternoon seen through the windows of this little room with the two beds and the two old ladies in it — three old ladies if you count Harriet, who is sitting by my bedside holding a magazine with a picture of a princess on it.

Are you sure you're all right? I say.

Yes, Mother.

She's a little irritated with me harping on her like that. She folds the magazine. The princess' face is cut off above the smile and she looks suddenly sad.

Do you know what eight nines are? I ask.

The bells stop ringing at last. The loudspeaker comes on, says ... something. Harriet's head snaps up, and she drops the sad princess.

The old lady in the other bed sits bolt upright and opens her mouth to shriek, you'd think she'd never heard an announcement before. She's short of breath, can't get much volume for her scream of terror. Someone tapes a piece of yellow paper to our room door, then rushes off. People have been rushing up and down the corridor all day. The loudspeaker tells us not to — not to something, worry probably, they usually tell us not to worry. I remember listening to a lecture in the lounge my first week here, an earnest young woman telling us all not to worry, that worrying was dangerous all by itself. Enough to make you worry even if you were healthy.

We wandered around Harbor Park all afternoon, Robbie and I. The first of two half-days off in a row that week, it was time away from my real self. Maybe for him too; maybe he didn't have many half-days off. He held my arm, pointed out ships on their way to England and South America that were loading, getting ready to head across three thousand miles of ocean with nothing in it but grey water and a few floating shells full of human hopes.

His car was parked on the street. He confessed that he'd

followed my tram to the park. By then I would have been used to his presence, his affection. I remember thinking, I could have saved a nickel.

And tomorrow's your birthday? Really? Happy birthday, Rose. Let me buy you something, he said. Let me buy you another drink.

I didn't say no. I didn't say no when the boys at school gave me sweets or apples, or sticks whittled into the shape of long thin dogs or long thin horses. I said, Thank you.

I should give you a real gift, he said. Maybe I'll get you something nice to wear. If I remember, he said.

He drove me home, walked me right up to the servants' door and said, Hello there, Parker. Who smiled a strange, sickly smile. I went upstairs to change and that night — that very night it would have been — I heard a knock at my door. A faint scratching, like a mouse behind the wainscotting.

What's wrong, I asked my husband, with what we've been doing?

It isn't any good for making babies, whispered Robbie from between my naked knees.

Why not?

Dr. Wilson says so.

You *told* him about us? Robbie! I'm mortified!

Would I have said mortified? Maybe embarrassed is what I said. I'm pretty sure I would have been both mortified and embarrassed.

I couldn't feel Robbie any more. Not in the usual way against me, a garter snake in the warm summer grass, inquisitive and then cautious. He was fumbling around with his hand.

What are you doing now? I asked.

Do you remember the blood just before Harriet was born? he

said, shifting against me on the bed so that his face was right by my ear. The blood on the ... um ... sheets, he said.

I nodded without speaking. I could feel his unshaven chin against my cheek.

The doctor asked what we ... did together. And when I told him, he ... he said that we've been doing it wrong, Rose. All wrong.

I didn't say anything. Inside I felt horrified. He knows, I thought. Dr. Wilson knows what we do together. Perspiration on my forehead. Also I was ashamed for doing it wrong.

Rose?

Yes, I whispered back.

Can you feel it when I do — this?

Harriet is sitting me up in my bed, an unusual vantage point. I feel clothesline. That's not it. I try to take in what's going on while I comb the tip of my tongue to find the word. Not clothesline. Nurses drop blankets on the two beds, disappear. The loudspeaker warns us not to worry. Are you worried? I ask Harriet. She shakes her head.

It's just a drill, she says. Nothing to worry about.

Sounds like my dentist.

Fire! Fire! Help, Mike. Help!

That's the sad lady from across the hall. Poor sad lady, she asks after Mike every goddamn day. Did I say that to You? Imagine — ungoddamn, then. Every single day. Mike is her son, and he died last year, some kind of car accident. He lived through the operation, and then died in the recovery room. The day after I found this out she came to our room and asked if we'd heard any news about her son's operation. She had such a hopeful look on her face I didn't know what to tell her. Such a strong boy, she said. Always in trouble on the playground. Stitches, we wouldn't believe. But what was a mother to do, a man was a man, you couldn't hold them back. He's a hawk, he should soar, she told us, and we nodded. One of the doctors led her away. A few seconds later a shriek of pure grief echoed through the wing. She knew. Once again, and with all the grief of first loss, she knew that her son was dead.

I think about this sad lady a lot. Every time she finds out about her son's death she collapses. Every time it's like the first time, and let me tell you it's awful finding out that someone you love is dead — listen to me telling You what it's like. You know, don't You?

I wonder why they keep telling her.

Robbie was getting a promotion, and the life insurance went with it. That's why he was seeing Dr. Wilson in the first place. It's Maple Leaf company policy, he told me, smiling at supper over a bouquet he'd bought on the way home. Yellow irises and begonia, I can still see the primary colours — *sorrow and passion* and *dark thoughts*.

Where did you buy these flowers, I asked, and how much did you pay?

It's a celebration, he told me, and pulled a bottle of legal whisky out of a brown paper bag. People are buying more Maple Leaf products than they have for years, he said. The company has made a profit for the last three quarters. The Depression is over, he said.

That's what the radio and newspapers were saying. Mind you, they'd been saying that for years and years and there still seemed to be hungry people hanging around outside the Zimmerman Bakery. Harriet liked waiting with the shabby men and women, sniffing the smell of fresh baking, and always seemed disappointed when we couldn't stay for the handouts. The women still smiled at her; the men still looked embarrassed.

Robbie's promotion had to do with him finding a new way to organize the Accounts Receivable, which when he explained it sounded a lot like Paid and Unpaid to me, but I'm no businessman. My accounts receivable at the flower shop were an embarrassment.

What about Harriet? I asked.

She can't hear us. She's asleep.

No, no, I mean — what about her birth? We couldn't have been doing it wrong.

I asked the doctor about that too. He said that there have been pregnancies that resulted from — what we do. But not too many. He said that this kind of — Robbie whispered the word in my ear, his breath heavy with the whisky — *sex* would explain the blood. Usually the blood comes when you ... when a woman ... does it the first time.

Oh.

Not during labour.

Oh.

Can you feel this? he asked.

I can't tell you how I felt when he crept out of the little upstairs room, my bedroom, closing the door so that it didn't click, creeping silently away. I lay in a kind of golden glow. The closest I can come would be to describe it as if I'd spent the time in Captain David Godwin's arms. His physical arms, I mean, not the imaginary ones I had used to feel all warm and girlish about. Mystical and perfect, of course, but ... at a loss too. There was so much to understand. Bewildered and transcended, I felt part of a larger whole. I had no desire to do it again. I could not walk around at the top of Mount Everest, or in the middle of a shower of falling stars. It was not a repeatable experience, and to tell the truth I do not know if we ever did repeat it. Were we doing it right? How would I know? I tell you we can't have been doing it wrong. I've never felt better. Scared, confused, but right.

That would have been when the baby was made. Must have been. On my birthday. And that must have been when the cufflink was left. Must have been then. I don't remember it, but that's natural, isn't it? Who would have noticed a man's shirt at a time like that?

A loud knock at the door in the middle of the night. Not Robbie's knock, and besides, he had a key.

Mrs. Rolyoke?

An official voice, hard to understand through the fog of sleep. Flashing lights from the street outside the house. It's dark.

Mrs. Robert Rolyoke?

Yes? I said, clutching my housecoat, peering out.

Was that my voice? It sounded more like Mama's. Yes?

Something terrible has happened, said the impersonal voice, from a long way off. A lot farther than the other side of the front door.

What happened? Is it Robbie — my husband? Is he all right?

My voice.

You must prepare yourself for the worst, ma'am. I'm afraid there's been an accident.

Soldiers die away from the field of battle. Traffic accidents happen in wartime. Soldiers on leave are still subject to the laws of chance and human nature. They die at the hands of careless drivers and jealous husbands and stick-up artists. They slip in bathrooms, get bitten by mad dogs, and succumb to fatal diseases. They get caught in machinery, burn to death, and fall out of things from great heights or at high speeds.

A policeman with a round red face sat on the chesterfield in our living room, holding his cap in his hands while he told me what had happened to Robbie. An embarrassed policeman. I would have been in shock, I suppose, worrying about whether I should offer him tea or a drink. Wondering about the correct reaction to tragic news.

This is what the policeman told me.

Robbie and young Sam were crossing Queen Street in front of City Hall around ten o'clock that Thursday night. Sam had been here to dinner — he was a shipmate of Robbie's, another sub-lieutenant. A nice young man from a small prairie town who wanted to see a bit of Toronto before going back to the ship. He had eaten an extra portion of macaroni and cheese, and an extra slice of canned meat. Harriet had eyed him all through dinner, fourteen years old she would have been, swooning with everyone else over James Mason and Lew Ayres. I suppose Sam did look a little bit like young Dr. Kildare.

Queen Street was empty at ten o'clock at night, except for a car with a very drunk man at the wheel. The car was stopped, and the man was trying to close a door that didn't want to stay closed. He tried with the window down and the window up, and every time he slammed the door shut it opened again, and he fell out of the car. Robbie and Sam — his full name was Sam Howe, he ended the war as a captain with a medal for valour — were waiting for an eastbound streetcar. They watched from the corner stop, applauding, as Sam told it later, at Robbie's funeral, when this unnamed drunk man finally got the door closed from outside the car. Realizing his situation, he ran around, but the door on the other side of the car — the only other door — was locked. He swore cheerfully, ran back, opened the driver-side door, got in, closed the door after him, and fell out when it banged open. The man lay on the pavement, his sides convulsing as he laughed.

Robbie and his friend decided to help. Sam got into the car and started the engine. Then he got out, and together he and Robbie bundled the man into the driver's seat. Then they slammed the door and stood back as the car lurched forward. A successful operation, only Robbie's coat was caught in the locked door. And as the car went forward so did he, knocking on the window to attract the man's attention. Which he couldn't. So he tried to take off his coat, still running beside the weaving backfiring car, slowly and then faster, my poor Robbie, while Sam stood open-mouthed in the middle of the street.

I can't smell smoke, I tell the nurses. Two of them, moving fast.

The nearer one calls me dear, tells me not to worry. She looks like a beet, round dark face, sprigs of hair at the top of her head.

The nurses take hold of the screaming lady's sheets, top and bottom, and make a hammock out of them. She stops screaming. They carry her away.

I call for Harriet. She's nearby. Doesn't reply.

The nurses return, move to the next bed as the doctor comes in. Not Dr. Sylvester, the other doctor. You know, he's handsome when he's worried, not unlike Dr. Kildare. A little darker, perhaps. What are you doing? he asks.

Transferring these patients, says the beet-headed nurse.

What's your name again? I ask the doctor. He flashes me a quick smile.

I'm Sanjay, he says. Well I guess he must be. He's got a million things to do. We've got to hurry, he says, if we're going to find room for them all on the bus.

Harriet steps forward, frowning. Taps the doctor on the shoulder. Enough room where? she asks.

What are you doing here? The doctor stares at her, like it was the first time. Almost a romantic stare, despite the wedding ring. And I suppose she is a bit too old for him. Harriet isn't used to romantic stares. I hope she knows what to do.

You should leave the building at once, he tells her. By the gate at the south end of the parking lot.

So this isn't a drill, she says.

He shakes his head. There is a small problem, he says.

Then a monster comes into the room, and Harriet screams.

Bluestone, I said into the telephone. What's this man Bluestone got to do with you?

Oh, Mother, if you only knew.

Well, tell me. I'm at Ruby's. Come on over for dinner. You can tell us both all about it.

My daughter's voice shook over the phone. She wasn't still trying to be a lawyer, was she? No, they'd changed the rules by then. She was working for the court of last resort — the office that sounded like it was from Holland. Come on over, I said. Ruby's making beans and back bacon. You always used to love that. We're trying a new ice cream flavour for dessert.

Early fall, that would have been. A lovely time of year. Windows open and the breeze blowing, still hot from the tops of the cars it had bounced off before coming through the apartment windows. Ruby's hat shop downstairs was shut. In the background I had the radio playing — I can't remember what it was playing. One of those songs that everyone sang all summer long and then forgot about.

Oh, Mother, I'd like to but I'm going out.

Someone new? I asked, and then, Sorry, none of my business. You're welcome to come by afterwards if you like. Both of you, I added.

Thanks, Mother. We probably won't — it'll be too late.

The radio switched songs.

The funeral service was well attended — several people from Maple Leaf, including an old man who made a point of telling me how much they'd all esteemed Robbie. That was his word. I thanked him. And Dr. Wilson, who sat at the back with the old ladies who live there — at least they've been there at every funeral I've ever gone to.

And Sam, in his sub-lieutenant's uniform. He sat beside us, young and respectable and pressed for time. He was on his way to Halifax right after the service. Harriet held his hand, sobbing mechanically.

It would have been just four of us at the graveside, me and Harriet, the preacher and the man from the funeral home. Windy and damp, but not raining. I remember the smell of the freshly turned earth. I turned around to look at the lake and saw him at once. How long would he have been there, I wonder. He wore an old black suit that fluttered and flapped against his thin straight body like a flag against a pole. He moved slowly forward as we went through the ashes and the dust and the committing of the body. His head was bare; top hat in his hand.

He stood beside the gaping mouth of earth and I saw suddenly how old he was, how old he must always have been. He did not speak. A shock of white hair blew off his forehead. His skin was translucent. His gaze was hard and searching, a blue-white predator's look. He peered through me, as if reading over the badly glued fragments of thought and feeling, the scrapbook of my mind, searching for — what? I don't know; I never could tell what he was thinking about. But I felt comforted. He put out a hand towards Harriet, who was sobbing at my side. She wore a beret, and her hair ruffled up around it as if the pale hand were a gust of wind. She looked up for a moment, her eyes bright and shiny with grief, then turned back to the coffin.

Amen, said the preacher. Amen, said Harriet. I threw a handful of mud into the hole. Goodbye, Robbie, I said.

A hideous misshapen head, eyes the size of saucers, and a coil coming out of its mouth, the monster reminds me of something. A human fly? I can't remember. It's not frightening, though. It's a comforting feeling. The rest of the monster is dressed like a doctor, white coat over an expensive suit. Familiar hands, soft, expressive, chilly. Dr. Sylvester's hands.

I smile up at him, but he beckons the other doctor out into the hall and starts talking about contingency plans. What does the institutional protocol say? he asks. What does it say about *triage*?

Sounds like a kind of hobby craft, doesn't it? With needles and sticks and special *triage* scissors.

All the downtown hospitals have protocols, says Dr. Sylvester behind his monster mask. To determine which patients get saved in the event of an emergency, and which patients are deemed to be ...

I strain, but I can't hear any more. Harriet, I say.

Don't worry, she says. Her eyes are narrow and she seems suddenly much bigger than me. Usually I have to remind myself that she's not still thirteen and scared; for weeks after the funeral she wouldn't cross the street, and who can blame her? Don't worry, Mother, she says. If I have to, I'll carry you out myself.

I got the tea habit from Lady Margaret and Mr. Rolyoke. They had it every afternoon, together as often as not. I got used to the smell, and then of course there'd be cups of it in the kitchen for us, together with wedges of bread and butter and jam. I liked the berry jams we had in the summers in Cobourg. The berries were local, and the jams had a lovely taste, so rich it was almost bitter.

Would you like some more tea? I asked the embarrassed police officer. He hadn't touched the cup I'd poured for him.

No, ma'am. Thank you.

You're sure?

Yes, ma'am. Twisting his uniform cap into a pretzel shape.

Very well. Go on, I said, with commendable firmness, only I

spoiled it by knocking over the sugar bowl, and then staring at the mess, my hand shaking like a loose window frame in a high wind.

He didn't see it, his eyes were on the floor.

And then, ma'am, the deceased — Lieutenant Rolyoke — your husband, ma'am — he found his coat was caught in the car door, and he couldn't get it off very easily. But he succeeded, ma'am. We have the other officer's — Lieutenant Howe's — evidence, and then the coat itself was located a bit further down Queen Street — still attached to the car door, ma'am, he added, his voice low.

Yes, I said.

Lieutenant Howe said that after running most of a block and wrestling his coat off like a ... a contortionist, your husband stepped safely away from the vehicle, which proceeded in a very erratic manner for a further fifty yards, finally climbing the curb and smashing into one of the large display windows of the Eaton's department store. Your husband had stopped, perhaps to catch his breath, and he was run over by another vehicle going the other way. I'm sorry, ma'am. Please accept my ... condolences on your tragic loss.

The poor officer wouldn't look at me. He stood up, said again that he was sorry, put on his cap, and walked out the front door.

My husband died during the war, I told Ruby. I wonder what she would have thought if I'd showed her the plot in the Woodbine Cemetery, halfway up the hill, facing south. From his grave I had a view of the lake, mind you I was standing up. I wonder if he could see it? Robert Rolyoke, 1910–1944. Around the stone I planted black mulberry — *I shall not survive you.*

I didn't know what to say when Ruby mentioned a cruise. Probably said nothing right away. I would have been too surprised. Then I said, No, pretty firmly.

I've never been on a cruise, I said. Not that I remember, that is. I came over from England when I was a baby, but I don't think I've even been in a rowboat since then. And whenever I used to think about Robbie, in that huge ocean, all by himself in the ...

I wouldn't have broken down, he'd been dead long enough, but I must have looked a little distraught. Ruby put her hand on my arm. Hey, she said. She was always a great Hey-sayer.

Hey, Rose, come on.

What about Harriet? I said.

I've already talked to Harriet. She thinks it's a great idea.

I don't know.

It'll be fun, she said. The Great Lakes in fall. Drifting through the Thousand Islands while the sun sets and the band plays — and you know these boats are always full of men.

Ruby!

Well, they are. You should be getting out more, Rose. You may be a widow with a daughter in university, but you're still a beautiful woman. You shouldn't be hanging around a dingy old flower shop all day long.

It's not dingy, I said.

Or waiting for Geoff Zimmerman, the baker. You looking for a bun in the oven? Hey?

Ruby!

She chuckled.

Geoff is kind, I said. He used to let Harriet and her friends go over there to practise. Poor people love him. You remember how he helped them out during the Depression, I said.

Sure, he's a saint, but he's sixty years old, and hairy. He'd look much better on a medallion, don't you think?

My shop is not dingy, I said. It's bright, and full of colour. And I see men all day long.

Men who are buying flowers for someone else. On a cruise you meet men who want to buy flowers for you! Men who love a good time.

Ruby! Are you serious?

Jump out of the frame, girl. Grow up and have fun!

But ... what about you? You're engaged, I said. Aren't you? What about Montgomery?

Whose picture I saw every time I went over, a very dashing nearlikeness in a silver frame, young man in a flying jacket and moustache, smoking a cigarette. Movie-actor looks, except for a nose which quested strongly to the left. Very obvious in person, not so much in the picture, which was taken at an angle.

Ruby's mouth closed into a thin red line. She looked away.

Monty and I aren't ... that is, we had a big argument last night.

I'm sorry, I said.

He yelled and I yelled and he stomped out of my place, and I broke a dish. Last thing he said was that he was going on a cruise. Without me. So I said that I'd go on a cruise without him, she said.

I'm sorry, I said.

For what? He's a bum. Monty Belinski. Could you see me as Ruby Belinski?

I never knew his last name, I said.

I don't know what I'm going to do, said Harriet.

We were eating lunch at a little restaurant on Bloor, around the corner from the museum. Harriet was letting the switchboard hold her calls and I was letting a hopeless young man look after my shop for a couple of hours. Hopeless in the business sense, not anything You'd be interested in. He was a long way from despair but he wouldn't add on the sales tax no matter how often I told him. It's only a few percent, I'd say, but it makes a difference. Yes, Ms. Rolyoke, he'd say, brushing the hair away from his face. His hair was longer than mine.

I owe Mr. Sherman some loyalty, said Harriet. I've worked there for a long time, and he did try to help me with my stupid law exams. But the firm downtown is offering a lot more money. And I'd have my own office. Law clerks don't usually get their own office, she said.

Is Mr. Sherman's wife still bothering you? I asked.

She made a face. Yes.

I chewed carefully. Tuna, it would have been. We were in an old-style diner that still served sandwiches with a side of slaw and a pickle. Harriet had a western sandwich, with ketchup. The sun shining through the big dusty restaurant window made a corner of the ketchup bottle sparkle like a diamond.

She calls my apartment at least once a week, wanting to know if Mr. Sherman is there, said Harriet. I don't know how she got my number. It's unlisted. I'll have to change it again, I guess. Last night she called, and Brian answered the phone. Mrs. Sherman told him to get out of the place now, and come home.

Who's Brian? I asked.

Oh, he's a friend.

That's nice, I said.

Forgive me, I was interested. At Harriet's age — what would she have been then, thirty-six? Not exactly a spring lamb. At her age I had a daughter in a wind band.

What do you think I should do, Mother?

I don't know, I said. I've never met Brian. What does he do for a living?

Oh, Mother! I wasn't talking about Brian. I'm not going to do anything about Brian. We're just friends.

She never paid any attention to me. No point in my saying, Leave Sherman and his crazy wife and go downtown and have an office of your own. Harriet would have done what she wanted to anyway. What can any mother do about her child's destiny? What did Your mother do? She worried, right? And suffered. And she cried over Your dead body. That's what mothers do.

The fire bells are still ringing. Ding ding ding, ding ding ding. If you close your eyes you can almost mistake them for the bell the streetcar rings instead of a horn. Or the sound of an old play-ground bell, swung by the teacher who wanted everyone to know that recess was over, and it was time to go back to the nine times table. Grinning farmboys with their chapped hands and oversized caps, nudging each other and joking about girls. And Jack, little dark intense Jack Dupree who looked at me out of the corner of his downwards-slanting eyes and paid compliments. I loved school, didn't I. Maybe that's why I resented Harriet's education, wanting what she had. I was so mad when she started practising over at Geoff's place. But you don't like me practising at home, she said, frowning. You called it an unholy racket.

And I did too. *Mea culpa.* What are You smiling at now? Ruby used to say that all the time. It means sorry, doesn't it? Sorry, Harriet. It was an unholy racket but I shouldn't have said anything. My daughter, I should have let you make your unholy racket.

I was angry because you made the racket at Geoff's place, amid the smell of fresh dough and cinnamon and butter and nuts and raisins. You went to the bakery after school to practise, while I worried about making a living and being lonely.

Would I have been lonely with Geoff? With his hairy floury arms folded across his broad front. A good player, this Harriet, he told me. She and her friends are welcome here any time. The bread rises better when they play.

Do you like Mr. Zimmerman? I asked Harriet, washing dishes together after dinner. She dried with lots of energy, as if she could polish the pattern right off the plates and cups.

Sure, he's nice. And he gives us cookies when we're finished practising.

Do you think he's nice looking?

Mother!

Sorry.

❧ ❧

Hello, I say, startled out of the past into the distant past. Hello, Daddy!

There there, says a monster.

Daddy put on his gas mask for me, once, just after he got back from The War. I giggled. I asked him to put it on again, but he never did, and after a while I stopped asking him.

What's going on? I say. What are you doing?

There there, Mother.

The monster has Harriet's voice. Two more monsters are bending over me, holding a monster face out towards me. I smile and reach for it.

Well, says the muffled voice of the nurse. That was easy, wasn't it?

I start to cough.

So we don't go on a cruise — we should still go someplace, Ruby said. How about a motor trip? Hey? We could drive down to the Adirondacks.

She leaned over the counter at my flower shop, waving a brochure in my face. I can see the brochure now, as brightly coloured as the autumn itself.

I don't think so, Ruby, I said. The people in the picture were sailing across one of the Finger Lakes. My hands sweated so hard I had to keep on wiping them on the side of my dress.

Come on, what are you afraid of?

I don't know, I said.

Leaving Harriet? Forget it! She'll be away at university. She'll be fine.

I don't know what I'm afraid of, I said.

Well, I'm damned if I'm going to stay in Toronto and sell hats to old ladies while Monty goes off somewhere and has a great time.

Okay, I said.

Okay? Okay what?

We'll go someplace. We'll go to New York, I said.

A customer came in then, a balding man who smelled like whisky and aftershave and, faintly, of mothballs. His glasses trembled on the end of his nose.

We're going to New York, Ruby told him, grinning from ear to ear. Rose and I are going to New York City. I can hardly wait to see the look on Monty's face, she cried, slapping the poor man on the back so hard he staggered forward and had to catch hold of the counter.

Do you have any ... gardenias? he said quietly, leaning over the counter.

Secret love.

Of course, I told him.

Something on my face. A mask. So you can breathe, the monster nurse tells me — I don't know why. I can breathe without it. Okay, I say. My voice sounds muffled. Like hers. She lifts a sheet to make a hammock for me to be carried away in. I look past her and there You are, wearing a mask like the nurse's. The bells are fainter.

I hear the other doctor talking to Harriet. Don't worry, Miss Rolyoke, he says. *Triage* is not part of Warden Grace Villa's institutional policy.

Harriet asks about contingency plans.

In the event of an emergency, the doctor says, our contingency plan is: Everyone gets out. Save everyone.

I hear birds and traffic noise, and the sun flashes in and out of my eyes as my hammock sways around. Harriet! I call. My voice sounds odd in my ears.

There there, says the nurse. Her voice sounds different too.

Outside. That's where I am.

Harriet, are you there? I call.

No answer. I start to cough.

I'm inside again, under a window. The bed throbs under me, so that I panic. I don't like the feel of a motor underneath where I'm sleeping. I don't like it. There's something about being in a bed, and staring out at the world through a moving window, that sends chills up and down my spine. I want help. Something's wrong. Mama! I call. Mama, Mama!

I dreamed; I don't know when this would have been, but I remember dreaming it more than once, waking up to tear-soaked lonely pillows.

In the dream Harriet, the little girl who scrambled and played and banged on pots and learned her ABCs, Harriet had gone off to play in the river — I wonder which river that would have been, there was no running water near the house on Waverley. The Cobourg Creek ran past the big house on the lake, maybe that's what I was thinking about. Anyway, she and a girlfirend went down to the river to play one afternoon, and the girlfriend comes back and tells me Harriet's dead. I run down to the water's edge and there she is, lying on the pebbles with her hair streaming around her. Dead all right. And I feel, in the dream I feel, such sadness. And the sadness continues as time passes in the dream. Pages torn off the calendar, leaves growing, turning, falling. I live in shadows, move slow, talk low, do the sad things. I don't think I can take it but I do, day by day. And then I go down to the water's edge — this would be the eastern beaches of Toronto, colourful but nearly empty in autumn — and I begin, very slowly, but perceptibly, to feel better. The colours are brighter, the boats are crisper, the breeze smells better — everything about the scene becomes more clear. I am getting back my life. Getting it back slowly. And I look up and down the practically deserted beach, and I pray.

We packed, Harriet for the term and me for the weekend. My suitcase and her trunk waited together in the shadows of the front hall. Harriet and I were in the living room, looking out at the street. We made the conversation you make when you're expecting someone any minute: Looking forward to your first — or would it have been her second year at university? Looking forward to it? I said. She nodded. A little scared? I said. She nodded. We waited and waited, departure times drawing closer and closer, and finally I called Ruby's place.

Who's this? said a strange voice.

Sorry, I must have the wrong number, I said, but before I could hang up I heard Ruby in the background.

Hey! Give me that phone, she said, and then, Rose? That you? Sorry I'm late — I overslept. What time is it? Is it really? Shit! Be right over.

Mother, did you remember to pack my music stand? Harriet called.

Uh huh, I said.

The man's voice on the phone hadn't belonged to Monty. Monty had a high nasal voice, and this one had been gruffer, deeper.

Am I pretty? I used to think I was. The boys at school told me I was. Girls used to envy me — sounds crazy, but they did. I could tell. And You want to know something even crazier? I liked it. Not just the boys' attention, but the girls' envy. It made me feel better about myself, as if they knew me better than I did. I didn't think I was worth envying. Robbie told me how beautiful I was. Mr. Davey did too, but in a gentlemanly way without words, just the way he looked after me, and smiled extra wide and got to his feet when I came in the room. It was part of my life, being pretty. And then, not suddenly, but in a kind of irreversible downward way, I stopped being pretty. Something I'd taken for granted, part of myself, wasn't true any more. No more compliments from strange men, no more whistles in the street, fewer and fewer envious glances from pretty women. It was like the gradual loss of use of a limb, there's a word for it, I know, because the next time anyone told me I was pretty, the next time after New York, would have been my very first month at the Villa, and he told me the word. He had lost the use of one of his legs.

Aren't you beautiful, he whispered, after lunch, in the room where they played cards and did jigsaw puzzles and stared into corners. Aren't you something, he whispered, wheeling himself over to where I stood, alone and faintly wistful, leaning on my walker. I knew what he was talking about and immediately — and I mean immediately — felt pretty again. As soon as the compliment was out of his mouth, I found myself turn with the same grace and charm I'd always had, to smile down at him with gratitude but not surprise. I'm Rose, I said. And this is my daughter, Harriet.

She didn't want to go, but I insisted. It'll do me good, I said.

How about if we go outside today, she said. It's warm and sunny.

I didn't want to go outside. I had something planned. The

Community Room, I said. They have tea there. You like tea, Harriet. And the milk comes in a silver jug, I said.

I know, she said with a sigh.

How does she know? I wonder.

There was an argument going on at the table nearest us, four crabby card players fighting about what they were going to play. I *said* clubs, I know I did, sobbed a man with a golfing cap and a hearing aid laid out on the table in front of him.

That was last deal, the others were saying.

Lead a card! said a fat lady with glittering eyes.

I'm Rose, I said to the man in the wheelchair, who had complimented me. And this is my daughter, Harriet.

Are you? he said.

I think so, I said.

You look like Mavis, he said to me.

What's your name? I asked him.

I'm Albert Morgan, he said. Don't you know me? I'm Albert.

I'm new here, I told him.

You sure look like Mavis, he said. You're so beautiful. If I wasn't in a wheelchair, I'd take you dancing.

And I smiled down at him, a not ill-looking man in a bathrobe and slippers. He had lots of hair, brushed all over the place so it might have been a forest on top of his head, or a field of dry wheat stalks blown by conflicting winds. His eyebrows were untrimmed, and hung down shaggily like Uganda — no, not Uganda, that's a place. Like ivory. No, that's not it either, but it's something like that. So much like it that I'll never get the right word. Bushy eyebrows he had, and hair on the backs of thin pale wrists. His legs were thin too. One of them moved around nervously, light, dancing movements.

Lead a card! commanded the fat lady at the card table.

The man in the cap was sitting next to her. He thumbed nervously through his cards. What's trump? he asked, in a loud voice. Is it clubs? Are clubs trump?

That was last deal, said the others.

If I wasn't in a wheelchair I'd take you dancing, Albert told me.

Isn't that nice, I said.

I used to be a pretty good dancer. I won cups. Then I lost the use of my leg.

Oh, I said.

The muscles atrophied. Now I can't hardly move it.

I never danced much, I said.

Sure you did.

I smiled. Not really.

Sure you did, he insisted.

Harriet was standing beside me, hand on my arm. Never opened her mouth. Poor Harriet, no social sense.

How come you have more cards than I do? complained the man in dark glasses. It's not fair, you all have four cards and I only have three.

Attention, everyone, I said, in my loudest voice. Attention everyone in the room. That means you too, I said to the card players.

Oh, Mother, said Harriet.

Ruby was a funny companion, commandeering a porter with a little metal whistle, giving Harriet an exaggerated teary send-off on her train to Kingston. Harriet actually smiled for the first time that morning. Then she asked if I'd packed her toothpaste. Goodbye, I said. You're a big girl now. That means no, doesn't it? she called over her shoulder, climbing the steps into the coach. Smart kid, my daughter.

Come on, now, Rose, you slowpoke, we've got to get to our train, Ruby called, sprinting off. I followed her wiggling hips as fast as I could.

A beautiful September day it would have been, far from rare, but precious all the same. Things don't have to be rare to be precious. Beauty and goodness are more common than you think; just look in any garden plot.

In our seats with our magazines and cups of Buffalo and Erie coffee, I asked Ruby flat out, Who answered the phone this morning?

She chuckled, unembarrassed. That was Clark, she said. My piano tuner.

But Ruby, you don't have a piano.

Who needs a piano if you have a good tuner, she said, hunting through her purse. Very sensitive fingers, she said. He needs them on his job.

Ruby! I felt obliged to act shocked. It made Ruby happier if she was shocking people.

Got a match? she asked. I don't seem to have any left.

You can have my attention any day, said Albert, smiling up at me, tapping his unwithered foot. You can have my attention and some more too.

Please, Mother, said Harriet.

I had their eyes now, all of them, the whole room looking at me the way you look at the television when there's only one channel. Nothing better on than me right now, so they were watching. Even the card players.

Good afternoon, ladies and gentlemen. I'm Rose and I'm new here. I have a short but important announcement to make.

Harriet stood beside me, head bowed, face locked in an expression of suffering. She hates to be made a fuss of.

I would like to present my daughter, Harriet, I said, turning slowly to starboard, like a ... well, like one of them. A big one. This young lady here, I said. She'll be coming by to visit me, and I want you to know her. Look well, I told them all, though the card players had gone back to their game. Albert was frowning up at me.

But you're not Rose, he said.

Come along, Mother, said Harriet. Tears in her eyes, she wiped them away.

You're Mavis, he insisted. You know, he wasn't that bad looking. For a skinny cripple.

Harriet and I found a table to ourselves. A stain on the cloth, but I didn't mind. Oh, Mother, Mother, she said. Where are you? She looked so sad, staring at me as if my eyes were windows with the curtains drawn, and she was trying to see past them into my living room.

Hi, there, said a lady in a sky-blue coat. A doormat — no. Haven't seen you two in a while, she said.

Do you know my daughter, Harriet? I asked her.

She smiled. Course I know Harriet, she said. Don't you present her to everyone whenever you come in here?

Harriet smiled sadly. Hello, Fern, she said. A volunteer. That's what Fern was.

Do you want a cup of tea, Mother? With milk from the silver jug.

I hate tea, I said.

4

Annunciation

The sound at the door was fainter than breath on a window. I knew it more than I heard it. Come in, I said, my own whispered voice ringing like a great bell. I strained my eyes in the pitch dark of the third-floor bedroom, wanting to see his face, his hand on the door, wanting to see the door opening. But I saw nothing, heard nothing but my own lungs pushing the wind away. Next thing I knew I was gloriously overwhelmed, as if by a huge and affectionate mythical beast. Or maybe I was a shivering bather, plunging my cold loveless body into water so steaming hot that pain and pleasure were one. I could not, cannot now, say what happened. Did we speak? I have neither sound nor picture in my mind, only a glorious series of sensations, a kind of sense-movie. How long it took I do not know, but the smell afterwards was very strong. Smoke.

He did say I was beautiful. I can hear it. I can hear it even now. Did he say anything else? Did he say goodbye? I don't know. But he did call me beautiful. Am I really, I said. Am I really beautiful?

And in the morning, there was the sun, and the wrapped box on the desk. Silver paper with a true-love bow and a note inside. A gift for me on my birthday.

You bet you're beautiful, sweetheart, said the man at the hotel bar.

My face must have registered shock like one of those meters you carry around to test if the connection is live. Ruby's mouth opened in a carmine O, fringed with teeth and leaking cigarette smoke and hoarse laughter.

Careful, Orville, she said.

The man looked put out. Already said my name's Wilbur, he said. And can't a man pay a compliment to a ... ahem, a beautiful lady like Rose here? Have another, he said.

Thanks, said Ruby, downing her manhattan — the perfect drink for our trip, she'd already called it. Numerous times.

I didn't mean you, said the man, Orville — there now, I've got me doing it — Wilbur, the nice faintly drunk young man from advertising. I meant Rose here, he said.

She turned serious. Rose *is* beautiful, isn't she? said Ruby. You are right, Orville. I'm glad the two of you are hitting it off so well.

I glared at Ruby, but she was already laughing at the man on the other side of her, a fat man with a loud suit and a drink in each hand.

Hi there, Dad, said a young voice behind Albert.

He grunted without turning round. Junior, he said.

The man was a younger version of Albert, tall and thin, long faced, large nosed, but without the hair. He was almost bald. I wondered what Harriet would make of him.

How have you been doing, Dad?

Fine.

Harriet wasn't with me this morning. She promised she'd come one day soon. I nodded to Junior. A nice young man with dandruff on his dark suit. I wondered how you could have dandruff without hair. Albert didn't introduce us, so I turned to go. Gracefully on my good leg, trailing my not-so-good one. Albert stopped me. Rolled his chair right at me. His eyebrows fell over his eyes, making his glance stern and reproving. I smiled over my shoulder, not coquettish or anything, but a woman's smile at a man who likes her looks. You know the one.

Where are you off to, Mavis? Albert asked me.

I'm Rose, I said. Remember?

You are a silly girl, Mavis, he told me. I turned away to hide my smile. It was a bit of a thrill being called a girl. Took me back.

Oh, Dad. Oh, no. Junior stepped forward to grab the back of his father's wheelchair. He smiled at me too, but not like his father. He was embarrassed. Come on, Dad, we have to go, he said, pulling the wheelchair around.

Goodbye, Albert called over his shoulder. See you soon, Mavis.

Bye, I said.

Aren't you going to say goodbye to your own mother? Albert demanded. Junior wheeled him away without a word.

At the card table the fat lady was writing something on a scorepad. The little man picked his hearing aid off the table and tapped it, the way you tap a microphone to see if it's working. He winced. It was working. The other lady was making faces at him. Funny faces, I thought.

The place was called Pierre's. Long and narrow, with a bar down one side and booths on the other side. A dance floor at the back, with a quiet band, or maybe the talk was loud. The bartender's name was Max. He pushed his hair around when he wasn't making drinks and emptying ashtrays. Wilbur was explaining his work to me and Ruby. I was listening. Ruby was flirting with the man on the other side of her.

Wilbur's job was breaking down the people who bought things into groups. If we know who you are, he said, looking at me, we know how to sell you our product. He smiled with nice teeth. He liked talking about his work.

Even if it's ... shoes, I said, trying to think of something I didn't want to buy right now. My shoes, bought that day in Broad's, Fifth Avenue, were killing me.

Don't you like shoes?

All right, not shoes. Oh ... wrenches, then, I said. Or a brace and bit.

We wouldn't try to sell you wrenches, he said. We wouldn't waste our time on you with wrenches. We'd try to sell you what you wanted. What you'd've bought anyway. Only you'd buy ours, instead of the other guy's.

Like Lux soap, I said, instead of Palmolive.

The interested look on his face went suddenly deeper. The difference between noticing a handsome man in the distance and having a handsome man come up and ask you for a light. Which brand of soap do you buy? he asked me.

Whichever is the cheapest, I said. Though I do like the advertisements for ... Ajax.

Ajax? He couldn't believe it. Ajax? The thundering hoofbeats getting louder and louder as the white knight gets closer to you.... Really, he said.

I nodded. I always see him as a stern man, I said.

Tough with dirt, he murmured.

But just, I said. And gentle underneath.

Ruby was talking to a bald man with a huge ring on his pinky. He wiped his forehead a lot, and he had a lot of forehead to wipe. The pinky ring flashed in the barlight.

Pardon me, Rose, but are you over thirty?

I stared. A woman doesn't answer personal questions, but I was flattered to think that the issue might be in doubt.

I am over thirty, I said. Though, really, Mr. — I mean, Wilbur — I can't see what business it is of yours?

My agency has the Ajax account, he said. Nationwide. I'm very ... I'm interested in my work. Over thirty ... well well, and of course you're under forty-five. And you're ... single?

Widowed, I said. It was getting easier to think of myself that way; it was on all the forms.

He nodded. Widowed lady, between thirty and forty-five, he murmured, wriggling a little. Do you ... pardon the personal nature of this question ... own your own washing machine?

I nodded. His eyes shut. There were little drops of sweat on his eyelids. It was pretty hot in the bar. In the back the musicians were playing something slow and sultry.

Perfect, he said. Just perfect. Do you want to dance? he asked, leaning towards me. I could smell his hair.

Wilbur, I said. I'm not like that.

Yes you are, Rose. He opened his eyes. Statistics is an exact science, he said.

Was I surprised to hear the noise at my door? I must have been expecting it, to have heard it, faint as falling snow against the heavy panels. I must have been privy to the plan. I must have known, acquiesced, at some point led him to understand that his presence was expected at my chamber door in the house where he lived.

My new room was not lovely, not large, not tidy, not well appointed. It sat at the back end of the third floor hallway, beside the broom cupboard, across from Parker's cosy little den. It had been a furniture storeroom, and it still smelled of rotting leather and lumber, and squirrels. The window was small and hard to open, and faced north. All the tower maids wanted it. It's not fair, said Mrs. Porson in her raspy voice, that Rose should get her own room. She hasn't been here as long as me!

Shut up, said Parker. Shut up the lot of you. Make me sick, you cackle on like a parcel of hens.

We were all in the back kitchen. You know, I can still smell the lamp black. And the soot from the fireplaces. And the polish we used on the shoes and leather.

But you promised *me*, pouted little Maureen, Parker's favourite. You promised, she said, standing next to the stout matronly house-keeper, staring up with her little-girl face. Ringlets, dimples, figure as tight and trim as a boy's. We all tried for boys' figures back then, heaved ourselves down with hawsers and wraps to avoid flapping.

You promised, Parky, she said, greatly daring. None of the rest of us would have called her Parky to her face.

Rose gets the new room, said Parker. Final. I have orders.

I stared out the window, disturbed because I was being singled out, because I knew what was going on. Because I didn't know.

The back kitchen window overlooked a lane leading down to the stables — garage, I should say, though there were horses there too, still. Mr. Davey was burning trash in a big bonfire. Snow fell, the fat stupid surprised snowflakes of early spring, which vanished as soon as they touched anything.

Orders, rasped Mrs. Porson. From who, I wonder?

Orders from Master Robbie, said Maureen, in a whisper I was meant to hear.

Shut up, Parker said again. My orders come from Lady Margaret.

He came to me that night. I heard him, bumping down the corridor. I sat up in bed, thinking, This isn't right. Excited, though, eyesight sharp, heart bumping around like a bee in a bottle, flesh atingle. The door was in the wrong place. What was wrong? Not used to the room. I listened as hard as a shrew listens in the dead of night, sensing the owl floating overhead. I swallowed. Wondered what it would be like.

I heard his voice, muttering. Hush, I wanted to shout. Hush, you fool. She'll hear you.

The door handle turned. The door opened inward. Was that right? I saw his shadow in the shaft of hall light. A hunched crooked shadow, moving forward inexorably. Was that right?

He called my name.

Mavis, he called hoarsely. Mavis, it's me.

The lady beside me in the bus with beds — the lady in the bed beside mine — has hair the colour of Maine lobsters. Cooked ones. There's a lot of it and it's spread all over the pillow. She's moaning again. All about her nephews and nieces not coming to see her. All about the tragedy of her life. Diabetes. Pollution. Kids today who don't know what they've got. Who don't pay attention. It's all happening to her. Babies that cost twenty thousand dollars. Babies that die of neglect. It's awful, the world is awful, and she can't stand it.

The nurse comes swaying over to us and says, There there. The bus turns a corner, sharply, and I slide a bit in my bed. The nurse steadies me. The lady beside me moans some more.

My daughter, I say, but the lady next to me doesn't let me finish, she's like an express train going right through to the end of the line, no matter who's waiting to get on.

Don't talk to me about daughters, she says. My sister has daughters, the ungrateful swamps. All they ever do is complain.

My daughter — I say.

One of them teaches family planning, she says. Can you believe it? A niece of mine teaching family planning!

My daughter used to work in the legal profession, I say. Titles, wills, statements of claim, all sorts of things.

Family planning, she says. Telling people how not to get pregnant. I asked her how she could do that. What do you say when they come to you for an abortion? I said. Thought that would shut her up, but it didn't. She smirked as proud as Lucifer.

My daughter isn't proud, I say.

And suddenly the old bitch starts to cry. I can hear these harsh racking sobs that come from down deeper than the varicose veins in your ankles. Way down deep. All my life, she says, I wanted children. I tried and tried, and I couldn't have them. All my life.

She turns away. I don't know how to comfort her. Can You help? You're right there. Maybe she'll listen to You.

And, by the way, how come some babies cost twenty thousand dollars, and other babies are thrown away? What kind of system is that? Don't look sad, that's no answer.

Rose, Rose, he said.

Hush now.

Rose, Rose, I want you so much. A widow with her own washer and dryer.

Yes, Wilbur.

His kisses felt odd. Not bad, but wrong. If there's a difference. His arms around me, dancing, had felt wrong too. I'd never ... I mean, even with Robbie I ...

Maybe it was because it was a hotel room. I'd seen enough movies. I knew what happened in hotel rooms. Knowing Ruby, I could guess what was happening in our hotel room right now. We were in Wilbur's room. Same hotel, different view out the window.

But — what are these? he said.

What do you think they are? What do they look like?

Not very experienced, Wilbur.

You're not supporting them the right way. Women with children are supposed to have underwiring — usually with girdles attached. Not that you need a girdle, Rose, you're as slim as a willow wand.

Thank you, I said.

But you should take better care of your profile. In a fitted garment with underwiring, you'd really stand out in a crowd. See — like that.

He showed me how I'd look, supporting me with his hands.

I've got one with underwiring at home, I said. It's uncomfortable.

He pulled me down onto the bed.

I was sitting at my dressing table, brushing my hair. Not much of it left, but I felt like brushing it. The nurse was making up my bed. I wasn't really sick yet, so I had a bedroom of my own at the Villa. Harriet was going to visit me any day now.

Snowflakes brushed against the windowpane, knocking softly, wanting to be let in. Like fingertips. I shivered.

Mrs. Rolyoke?

Yes, dear. I turned my head away from the window. The nurse had a belt in her hand. Striped and made of ketchup — I mean terry cloth. A man's pyjama belt.

Is this yours, Mrs. Rolyoke? she asked.

I knew what to say. I kept my face still and said, I don't know.

I just found it in your bed.

I don't know how it got there, I said.

It belongs to Mr. Morgan, doesn't it?

The whole scene was a dream. I knew I'd been here before. Don't know, milady, I said.

The night nurse said she saw him coming out of your room last night. Do you ... know anything about that, Mrs. Rolyoke?

About what? I said.

I made my face blank. And after a moment she went away.

Harriet was embarrassed. So was the bald young man sitting next to her. I suppose he couldn't use the shampoo that stops dandruff, because he didn't have any hair to wash.

I remembered then, the young man was Albert's son. Albert called him Junior. We were sitting on a bench in a meeting room — me and Harriet and Junior. Albert rolled back and forth in front of us, like a duck in a shooting gallery.

A lot of people think I remind them of someone, I said. Remember that man who thought I was Gene Tierney?

Mother, please.

Standing in front of the Woolworth store on Bloor Street, and he wanted my autograph. Remember?

Yes, Mother. But Mr. Morgan here doesn't think you look like his wife. He thinks you *are* his wife. And you seem to ... to welcome his attention. Don't shake your head like that, Mother, it's true. The nursing staff have noticed.

I wasn't shaking my head to disagree, just to get my hair out of my eyes.

It's wrong, Mother. I want it to stop.

Junior nodded his head emphatically. You don't do any good playing along, ma'am, he told me. My dad's not playing around.

I'm sorry to say it but he's not. He really does get people mixed up with ... my mother.

Never mind, I said, reassuringly. I'm always getting people mixed up. Just yesterday I called someone a cyclamen, would you believe it. She was so upset. I told her, cyclamen is diffidence and modesty. You should be relieved, I could have mistaken you for a columbine.

They all looked puzzled. I tried to remember what I'd just said. Couldn't. I smiled brightly at Albert, who was bent over with his head on one side, trying to look up my skirt. Silly man.

That nightmare again. The horror of a child lost in the water. I ran down the path to the water's edge, and up and down the beach, feeling the pebbles underfoot, hearing the wash of the waves. I stared and stared until my eyes were sore and red, frantic with worry, wondering what had happened, was it even now not too late to somehow alter what had happened.

Mama Mama Mama.

I heard the cry, very faint but persistent. I'm here, Harriet, I cried. Harriet, is that you?

And there was her body, lying dead, just like her friend had told me. She was dead, and the water poured out of her mouth. Mama mama mama.

And I realized that I was the one calling out.

Oh God, oh that's good. Oh my God, he said.

Oh Orville, I said.

He paused.

I mean Wilbur. I wish Ruby hadn't started that.

Tell me what you're thinking, he said. Tell me what you want me to do.

I ... don't know, I said.

Do you feel that? he said.

It was dark in his hotel room, and I couldn't see what it was.

And that? He was panting, his body slick with sweat.

Very nice, I said politely.

One hand I felt, milking in vain. None there since Harriet, and that was quite a while ago. She was off to college now, studying political science. Wilbur's other hand was lost in darkness and chenille, until —

Hey, I said.

Did you feel that?

Oh, yes.

Wilbur's voice came from far away. Liked that, did you?

I didn't reply. He went on moving his hand, if that's what he was doing.

I was in a pitch-dark cave of feeling, pierced by an unexpected shaft of light when the sun hit exactly the right angle. I was aware of splendour and wonder, veins of delight. How long had they lain there, unnoticed? I was the possessor of great riches in myself.

The sound of water was everywhere, dripping and plashing. I was filled with longing. The water streamed down the walls, pooling at my feet. I arched my back to breathe deeper, and the water fell faster and faster, filling the cave, bearing me up and up. I felt my lungs expanding, as if they would burst. I felt ... I felt ...

Who, Wilbur asked later, as the cigarette smoke spiralled ceiling-wards, is David?

I saw him, then, smiling, bandaged, just as I remembered him in 1925. He hadn't aged a bit. Well, he wouldn't, would he?

Wilbur was lying propped on one elbow. His hair had fallen

damply over his forehead. He pushed it back. Didn't you tell me your husband's name was Robert?

It was, I said.

Uh huh.

I felt I owed him something. David was ... from a long time ago, I said. Before my husband.

He didn't say anything more.

The bus stops suddenly. I can hear the hiss of the brakes. Are we there yet? I ask. Are we home? Mine is not the only voice. We're like a flock of little birds with our mouths eagerly turned upwards, waiting to be fed. Wispy feathers, chirpy voices. Plaintive, needy, worried. Poor little birds

The nurses smile and stroke and reassure. Another couple of hours and we'll be able to go back. The chemical spill is all cleaned up, and they're moving the residents back into the neighbourhood. Don't worry. Don't worry.

Wait — who's that holding Your hand? Is it what's her name who's always calling after her dead son? She looks so happy. Big hard working hands on her, I see.

I beckon the nurse, whisper in her ear. It's been a while since I heard that lady shouting for Mike, I whisper. She's very quiet now.

Yes, says the nurse. She is.

The waiter had a big white apron and a big white smile. He looked flustered, talked quickly, forgot things. The outdoor café was set up as a medieval fair, with tents and pavilions and a big open kitchen. Harriet ordered sangria for us both.

What is that? I asked.

A red wine drink with fruit juice and other sweet things.

You'll love it, said the waiter, spilling some on the tabletop, wiping it up awkwardly with a dirty white rag, smiling again. So seasonal. A sunny summer day in Spain. He gestured around him. In 1400 A.D., he added over his shoulder, moving swiftly away.

So what's your news? I said to Harriet. Let me guess.

No, she said. Don't guess.

Almost fifty years old she'd have been, then, and still not married. What did it say about her? What did it say about me? I know how old she was because the subject came up later.

Let me tell you, she said.

I took another sip of the wine.

I've got a new job, she said.

You're not working for the lawyer any more, I said. The man with the awful wife and the voice from the radio. My dear Mrs. Rolyoke, he told me at a Christmas party some years before this, your daughter has told me so much about you I feel I know you already.

That's good, I said now, drinking my sangria. I never liked him.

Oh, I'm still working for Mr. Sherman —

The Velvet Foghorn, I said. Laughing.

Harriet laughed too, even though she'd heard my little joke before. I'm still working for him, but he's left his law practice to become the new provincial ombudsman. I'm one of his investigators.

What about his wife? I said. Does she still bother you at home?

No, said Harriet gently. Frank — Mr. Sherman — is divorced. She wasn't blushing. I'd have been blushing, in her shoes.

I was thinking, for some reason, of Holland. I suppose ombudsman made me think of Holland. It sounded like a foreign word. Where will you and the Velvet Foghorn be going? I asked her.

Harriet didn't understand my question. The ombudsman is a government office, she said. Like a cabinet minister. I work around the corner from where I used to.

The waiter came by, eager to know what I thought of the wine. His eyes were brown behind thick glasses. His apron had stains on it.

It's fizzy, I said.

That'll be the ginger ale, he said.

Mr. Cuyler came from Holland. And Mr. Groenveld. Big strong men with hands like steam shovels and appetites to match. They farmed over by Colborne way, down County Road 9, which was north of Precious Corners up by Plainville. Dairy cows, maybe a field of red corn, but it was fruit and flowers they made their money on. You want Dutch blooms, they said to the ladies in Colborne, in Grafton, in Campbellford and Cobourg and Port Hope, real blooms like on the box of Dutch Boy cleanser? Or was it motor oil? There was a Dutch boy on the cover, blond and blue-eyed with those pointed wooden shoes. Mr. Cuyler and Mr. Groenveld wore boots.

You want some fruit? they asked Mama, who said no.

Or flowers? Shrubs, or little trees, in front of your house would look very nice. Mr. Groenveld was talking. Mr. Cuyler was eating an apple. Three bites and the apple was finished. I stared. He tossed the core away and reached for another. Mr. Groenveld could eat three whole pies at a sitting; I'd seen him in a contest at the fall fair.

Daddy was out with Victor the horse, trying to clear rocks out of a field.

I went up to the cart. Wooden slats with dirt leaking through, fragrant with dung and pollen. Bushel baskets of fruit. Shovels resting beside buckets of water. I would have been nine or ten. Used to being poor. Used to disappointment, but able to recall hope.

No, thank you, she said.

Or seeds, they said. Cheap. Their wooden cart was piled high with colour. Insects followed them around all summer long.

Please, Mama, I said. They're so pretty.

Mr. Groenveld was older than Mr. Cuyler. He had white hair. His daughter was Mama's age. She was married to a man with one arm who ran the post office in Colborne.

Five cents for a spill of seeds, said Mr. Groenveld. Phlox, lobelia, carnations, and some others I don't remember.

Please, Mama, I said. Oh, please.

No, thank you, she said. Mr. Groenveld shrugged and backed up his horse.

Mr. Cuyler offered me an apple. I held it in my hand. I was hungry, and the apple smelled beautifully sweet. Thank you, I said, but I didn't eat it. I stared at the cart full of flowers. And at the twisted paper of seeds in Mr. Groenveld's hand. I knew the connection between them. I knew what happened when you put seeds in the ground.

What's wrong, little girl, said Mr. Cuyler. You don't like apples?

I wanted the apple, but I wanted the seeds more. I saw the flowers in my mind's eye, covering the ragged front of our farmhouse lawn. It was a slow dusty morning in early summer, and the clouds in the high blue sky looked like white dots.

You like flowers? he said. I nodded, and held out the apple, ready to trade present fruit for future beauty. He nodded his understanding, smiled and then reached into his cart for another twist of flower seeds.

Here, he said, nodding

No, said Mama. My mama.

No, Rose, you can't take it. Thank you, Mr. Cuyler, but we don't want any flowers or fruit today.

But —

Good morning to you.

What it cost my mother. She was proud, often talking about her family in the fen country, on the east coast of England. There was a cousin who was a lawyer in Ely. What it cost her to deny me my gift. What it cost, later, to ask for help, for food. Our neighbours were so good, so tactful, I never noticed that we were begging. Mama accepted help for the necessities — getting to market, food when there was none, or none but cabbage. But she wouldn't take help for frivolity. She never wore new clothes. I never had a toy, except the dolls Uncle Brian brought when he was doing well. Blue eyes and red cheeks and hair I combed until it fell out.

Mr. Cuyler went up to my mother and spoke to her in a low voice. He jerked his head at me. She shook her head. Mr. Groenveld backed the cart around and stood at the horse's head, waiting. The two of them were alike, tall and well made, strong and quiet, waiting patiently. I couldn't help noticing that Mr. Cuyler slapped at himself while he was speaking to Mama. At his clothes, his shirt and pants. He took off his hat and slapped it all over his jeans. Dust rose off of him in clouds. Nervous around women, I guessed. I stared at the farm cart. DUTCH BLOOMS said the sign on the side. Would I have been able to read it yet, or am I remembering another year? CULTIVATED BEAUTY.

Goodbye, sir, I said to Mr. Cuyler.

Come inside now, Rose, said Mama.

Yes, Mama, I said, but I turned back when Mr. Cuyler called my name.

Pray for rain, he said in a low voice, staring up into the almost clear blue sky and slapping himself.

All right, I said. And I did, that night. I almost forgot, but I remembered just before I went to sleep. The clouds were scurrying past the open window by then. We prayed for rain together, David and I.

Harriet wide-eyed and shouting at the foot of my bed. Sunshine slanting down the wall to hit the empty breakfast tray.

Are you all right, Mother? Did he hurt you?

Who? I said.

That bastard — I'm sorry but that's what she said. You know.

Who are you talking about, dear? I said, blinking up at her. Harriet is so passionate — funny word to use for an old spinster like her. She gets upset about things, I mean. That's passionate too, isn't it? She wasn't angry at me this time, was she?

You know who, she said. That disgusting old man. Morgan.

I frowned. You mean Albert?

Bastard, she said.

The sun was in my room in the mornings, and in the common room in the afternoons. I wasn't the only one who liked it. Others would follow it around the room like me, sliding their chairs over. I wore a sweater these days, old wool cardigan with buttons made in the shape of ... of those things with ... those things on them. Forks. No, not forks. Anyway, it was winter — last winter — and Harriet was angry and upset about something.

His son is talking to him now, she said.

Junior?

How can you be so calm? The Villa is upset. There's a committee dealing with the problem. I suppose it's the sort of thing you should expect in a place like this, but apparently it's not that common. There have been some cases in the United States, but they've never seen it here before. You and Albert are the first.

Are you sure you don't want a cup of tea? I asked.

I know they can't watch you all the time, but still! Are you feeling any after-effects this morning?

I decided to try to be candid with Harriet. She was my daughter; she'd understand.

What are you talking about? I said. She was so upset.

She was always getting herself upset about other people. When she got the investigator's job, she used to take files home with her, pore over them, write out life stories for the people involved, when they first experienced pains in their lower backs. We are the court of last resort, she told me. The people's choice for representation. I used to laugh at Harriet's boss, calling him the Omnibus Man, but she took it all very seriously. Even — now what was his name, forget my own next. Even money, eventide, even Stephen. That was it. Stephen was a crusade. Cost her the job, but she wouldn't change her mind.

He can't walk! she told me, pounding her hand on the table so hard the sangria spilled. My daughter. Sometimes I want to hold her and rock her until she stops crying. His legs and lower back are wrecked, she said. He's in a wheelchair and it's his company's fault and they won't pay. I'm his case officer. I've talked to him. I've talked to his doctors. I believe him, she said. We must get him a settlement!

Light blue eyes wide open, staring, passionate. Her father's eyes. My own are hazel, brown with flecks.

Stephen Bluestone was a forty-nine-year-old spackler, injured on the job two years back and hadn't worked since. He's my age, Mother, and he may never walk again! cried Harriet. He blamed the injury. The Workmen's Compensation Board didn't believe him. I didn't know what to think myself; it was all I could do to believe that spackling was a career.

He appeared several times before the Workmen's Compensation Board and the Ministry of Labour. He took his case to the newspapers. Well-meaning friends organized a petition that didn't get signed by very many people, and a rally on a day that rained. The Workmen's Compensation Board didn't change its mind. Stephen Bluestone took his case to the ombudsman's office.

We're his last hope, said Harriet.

It rained enough to soak the ground thoroughly. Then the sun shone. Then it rained some more. Then the sun shone again. A lovely summer for farmers: warm, wet, sunny. The hay grew too fast and wouldn't dry properly, but everything else did well. Fruit and green vegetables grew quickly, and did not get blasted by storms. The corn was taller than me before school was out that year. From the top of the hill next to Gert's place you could see for miles in every direction; all around the land looked in good heart.

Closer to home, the cabbages were good and big, the root vegetables came up well, and the stunted twisted trees at the far end of the north field bore fruit — the only time in my memory they did so. Small reddish-brown apples, soft enough to bruise easily, bitter to the taste. Gert turned up her nose at them, but I ate enough to feel sick.

And the gravel beside the drive, and the muddy ruts themselves, turned in the course of the summer into a confused little puddle of colour. Flowers of several kinds, an odd and brave display. Not lavish but not pathetic — something from nothing is never pathetic. I thought it was a miracle at first. Then I remembered Mr. Cuyler telling me to pray for rain.

I ran from bloom to bloom, sniffing. I traced their shape into the dust. I wove them into my dreams at night. I copied them into the school notebooks I'd brought home for the summer. I asked Mama what the names were, what kinds of flowers they were. She didn't know.

Parker crept around cat-footed, the spying, tale-bearing old biz-zom that she was. I found her leaning against the bathroom door, late on a winter's evening when I was returning with our scuttle of coals. Are you ill? I said, and she jumped out of her skin.

No, no, she mumbled, straightening herself out. She'd come undone, a rarity for her. Our bathroom was way out of sight and mind, an upper-floor boxroom with no running water. Nothing to hear or see there for her, with us off duty and getting ready for bed. It was cold too. Maureen was shivering when she came out. Silly to wash your hair as much as she did; you're just asking for pneumonia.

Get to your room this instant, I told her. The new girl is making up the fire.

One scuttle for all three rooms, Parker reminded us, turning to go back downstairs.

I heard her outside the bathroom door, gasping away, said Maureen in a whisper when Parker had gone.

☞ ☜

Breakfast at a cheap New York hotel in September 1949 — bacon and eggs, biscuits and coffee — was fifty cents, so we went down the street to a diner and had the same thing for two bits, which was still a lot. Ruby was hungover, to my relief. I didn't want to talk.

The woman in the booth behind me kept saying, Didja see ... to someone who never replied. Not once. Didja see that China ... that the mayor ... that the Giants ... that the garbagemen ... I turned around to see who it was ignoring her, but she was alone. Maybe she was talking to me. I smiled. She looked through me. Maybe she was talking to You.

Ruby slopped coffee into her saucer.

Oh my God, Rose, she said. Oh my poor Montgomery.

What?

She frowned down at the newspaper in her hand, reading intently.

Is it about China? I said.

She scrambled out of the booth. I have to phone, Rose, she said. I have to phone right away. Remember Monty's cruise? Well, he was going on the *Noronic*, she said.

I knew the name but couldn't remember where from. So? I said.

Hello, everybody, I said from my bed, glad I had thought to brush my hair before breakfast. You never know when you're going to have to look your best. No one said hello back. I tried again. Hello, Dr. Sylvester. I smiled up at him. What a dresser. Ruby would have loved him, except I wonder — funny now that I come to recall — I wonder if she liked Jews. She was cold and distant when she talked to Mr. Fleisher from down the street. We never talked about religion, but she called Mr. Fleisher a pushy guy — You know, the way they are, she said. I'd never had any clothing made to measure so I said I didn't know the way they were, but maybe she wasn't talking about tailors.

Dr. Sylvester nodded at me. He looked embarrassed. He started talking to the people next to him, a man in a hurry and a pregnant lady in a suit. The announcement came over the intercom: *Good morning, everyone. Today is Tuesday the third of March.* Pause. Then the year. Was it just last year? The pregnant lady smiled at me then. The lady on the other side of her from Dr. Sylvester whispered something in her ear, and she nodded.

Harriet sat on the bed next to me. She patted my hand. She looked embarrassed, like Dr. Sylvester and the night nurse. There was a feeling of embarrassment throughout the room, faint but definite, like the central heating.

Shall we begin? said the man in a hurry.

I'm sorry about the people on the *Noronic*, the hundred and some-thing men and women and children, but I didn't think about them at the time. My face would have gone as white as a sheet I'm sure — and I said to Ruby, Sank? It sank?

She wasn't thinking about the hundred and something dead either, only about Montgomery. She handed me the paper and ran to the back of the diner, hips wobbling under her burnt-orange skirt, rummaging in her purse for change for the pay phone.

Bottom of the front page, with a big headline: HARBOR TRAGEDY! FIRE ABOARD LINER KILLS ONE HUNDRED! I read the arti-cle all the way through, with my thoughts whirling like falling maple keys — bravery, death, destruction, Pier Nine, fruitless, evening dress, worst, authorities, inquiry, captain, second deck, wastebasket — no, wastebasket was later.

And relief.

That it wasn't me? That I didn't know anyone? No.

I was relieved that it was a fire.

You think of maritime disasters, you think of sinking. You assume the ship went down. That's how people die when they're onboard ship. That's the chance you take when you cross that rope bridge at Southampton. Or wherever. Air disaster, you assume: it fell out of the sky. There are other kinds of air disasters, but that's the one you think of first. It's the one you are afraid of. No one is afraid to fly because they think the plane is going to get caught in an earthquake.

It was like the way Robbie died. Soldiers die in traffic accidents. Boats catch fire. Survivors of Hiroshima get knifed in strange beds. Miners die of old age.

I know, said Parker, in a hoarse whisper, nodding her head like a marionette. I know.

What do you know? I replied. Breakfast time — for them. We'd already had our bread and jam. In the dining room they had sausage and bacon, eggs three ways, cold black toast smeared with butter. And coffee. I loved the coffee — always tried to steal a cup for myself. Some of the servants were always taking food, or liquor, but I never bothered.

I know what happens, said Parker. When she nodded, her cap frill flipped up and down very gracefully. I know what happens at night in your room.

Oh yes?

You think you're being so quiet. I listen, you know. Got keen ears, old Parky, don't you think, Rose, my girl?

Keen as mustard, I murmured, gliding a tray onto my arm and carrying it out through the swinging doors. I didn't know what she was talking about.

She came back to it that night. Getting ready? she asked as I was on my way to the bath.

I nodded. Chilly in the hallway and all I had on was a loose shift. Nightgown under my arm, yawning. Her eyes were bright with mischief.

Oh to be in your slippers, she muttered. Not that I suppose you're in slippers with him, hey?

I smiled, unsure of her meaning.

I don't want to tell her ladyship about it, she said to me, putting her hand on my shoulder. It reached all the way around, to grab my shoulder blade, like a claw, or the tines on a pitchfork.

Tell her what? I asked.

That's it. Keep up the front, she said, squeezing.

I moved past her to the door of the bathroom. The hot water steamed invitingly.

You know, I've a fancy for a bath myself, said Parker, staring at me and then at the water, which I'd carried up myself from downstairs a few minutes ago.

I —

I think I'll take my bath right now. Parker took the towel from my hand and stepped over the doorsill.

I shouldn't have protested. I should have smiled and nodded, and left the room, but I stepped up to her and said, It's my turn.

She was already unbuttoning herself. It's my turn, I said again. I was whispering, I don't know why. It was ridiculous, but it was also embarrassingly intimate.

You've always hated me, I said. I shivered.

Haven't. She stared at me, breathing hard. Haven't.

I stepped back, but it was a small room, and Parker and the hot water bucket took up a lot of space.

We'll have a bath together, she said. You can go first if you like, since you brought up the water. I'll jump in after you, Rose.

I blinked.

I don't hate you, she said. You're young and beautiful. No figure, mind you, but you are quite beautiful.

She stared at my — at my figure, I guess. I blushed, and pulled my robe tighter.

Remember, I know about you and him, she whispered. And her ladyship doesn't — yet.

Reaching forward, she stumbled and fell against me. I smelled liquor on her breath.

The driveway dragged on and on, people talking to each other with smiles on their faces, making notes on their ... things you make notes on, Harriet patting my hand. Mostly she looked angry but once I surprised a look of pain on her face, after I'd said something to the man in a hurry. He wasn't a doctor, he was too tall and too badly dressed. He chewed mints all the time, like he was trying to give up smoking. Did I say driveway? I meant meeting.

You don't understand, I told him. Albert is a friend of mine. Don't you have any friends?

He didn't reply. Dr. Sylvester, he said, in your opinion is this guest — we were all guests at the Villa, isn't that a nice way to put it? Like the Villa was a hotel. Except that we weren't getting out of the hotel alive — is this guest competent to make her own decisions?

Dr. Sylvester cleared his throat. Rose, he said, smiling at me, is a charming and occasionally lucid person.

Thank you, doctor, I said.

Her daughter and I have discussed the issue of her competence. As of yet Harriet has made no decision. Which means that —

Legally, interrupted the pregnant lady.

— Yes, legally, Rose is still competent.

Everyone looked down at me. They were all on their feet. I was in bed, like royalty. I waved.

We have no right to forbid consenting adults, began the pregnant lady.

On hospital premises, said someone else.

They had said this before. I looked at Harriet and rolled my eyes. She wasn't bored, though. She was upset.

Don't you see, she said. I want my mother protected from ... attacks.

They didn't ignore her. I was glad to see that.

But, Miss Rolyoke, they aren't attacks if she gives consent, said the lawyer. We have no right to restrain Mr. Morgan from ... visiting someone who's expecting him.

It's ludicrous. He calls her Mavis, for heaven's sake.

Harriet's lip quivered.

Don't hate me, I whispered to her. Please don't hate me.

Oh Mama. I'm so scared. I can feel your heart beating fast and light, and I'm so scared. The birds in the cage overhead are shrieking.

In the distance I can hear the sound of rushing water.

Saturday brunch in midtown Toronto. Winter's slushy fingers grabbed at the city like a visiting brother-in-law, whining that it was only a few weeks and then it would be gone. For good, this time. The medieval tents had all been taken down, the pavilion turned into an ice rink. No one skated; it was too wet. Harriet and I were inside, drinking coffee.

Would I? Would I have had a drink instead of coffee? I might have. It's not a sin, You know. On a Saturday afternoon, a recently retired lady listening to her daughter's troubles at work can have a drink.

Good news, she told me. Mr. Sherman thinks Stephen is telling the truth. We're going to be able to get his case heard again by the Workmen's Compensation Board.

That's wonderful, I said.

I just hope we can make the board change its mind. The medical reports are tricky. The orthopedic surgeons all say he's faking, and his chiropracters all say he's telling the truth.

Have you followed him? I said.

She took a sip of coffee before answering. Why would I follow him, Mother?

She's so smart, Harriet, she doesn't know how she puts up with me sometimes.

Well, you're an investigator, I said. And following is what investigators do. Sometimes. I was thinking that if you followed him you might find him tap-dancing or something. And then you'd know he was faking.

Harriet smiled, the way she does when she's exasperated. A truly frightening smile, I think it's why she never married.

Mother, I work for the government of Ontario. The ombudsman is a civil servant, not a private detective. I read files and interview doctors.

Oh, I said, sipping my — my drink, I guess. Hope it wasn't rum. I'd drunk it with Ruby, but never really liked it.

And I don't think he's faking it, Harriet said thoughtfully, staring past me. I've spoken to injured workers' groups and to the Workmen's Compensation Board about Stephen, she said. No one thinks he's faking the pain. They just don't know what causes it. It's hard to prove that the whole thing is related to his job. The X-rays are inconclusive, she said.

Big greasy snowflakes fell straight down onto the empty skating rink. Icicles hung from the boughs of plastic pine trees in pots. Despite the slushy conditions the icicles did not drip, and I realized that they were artificial as well, fastened with metal bands to the boughs of the artificial trees.

Is he a good-looking man, this Stephen? I asked.

Mother!

No, really.

She sipped her coffee and looked away. Well, then, yes, I guess he is. If you like the type.

⌒ ⌒

Now Parker had it in for me. She had me washing up for three days in a row, instead of alternating between the four indoor girls. The back kitchen — scullery, they called it — was windowless and chill, with a stone floor. At least the water was hot. Maureen offered to take my job on my birthday morning, but Parker insisted, glaring at me spitefully.

I asked Mr. Davey what I should do.

We were in the coach house, around the back. I was in my walking dress, so it must have been an afternoon off. He was polishing the Hispano Suizo. He drove Mr. Rolyoke downtown to work in the mornings, and then drove back to the house by himself. In the afternoons Mr. Davey drove downtown by himself, and back to the house with Mr. Rolyoke. There was a smaller car in the garage, I can't remember the kind, and a cabriolet Packard that Lady Margaret used. I saw the cars every morning: both the Hispano and the Packard had flower vases in their passenger compartments.

Do you know why Parker should be persecuting you? he asked.

I hesitated, then told him as much as I could about the incident in the bathroom.

He was concerned. Did she hurt you, Rose? he asked.

I flushed, recalling the lurch of her heavy body in the dim light, the shock of her hands on me. I didn't know she drank, I said.

Mr. Davey didn't say anything. He knew, I suppose.

Why don't you talk to her ladyship, he said, wiping away water spots from the front fender. Tell her the problem you're having with Parker.

I hesitated. I don't know if Lady Margaret really cares for me, I said. Inside the garage was a smell of horses, left over from the last generation. Comforting, somehow. Outside, the rain beat down.

He didn't say anything. He knew why. I suppose it must have

been the gossip of the servants' quarters, even though no one had ever said anything directly to me.

There you are, Rose. I've been looking all over for you.

Robbie stood in the doorway, hands on his hips. A cigarette stuck out of his mouth at a jaunty angle.

Good afternoon, sir, I said.

That's a nice scarf you're wearing, he said with a sweet, innocent smile. Who gave you that? It looks like real silk.

Mr. Davey kept his head down, polishing.

Who died on the *Noronic?* Passengers, that's who. The crew were all ashore. You wouldn't think it would be so bad — ship catches fire in the harbour, all the people had to do was hurry ashore — but the fire was on the shore side. Some people swam to safety, but a lot didn't. Lake Ontario is awfully cold in September.

Ruby and I arrived back in Toronto the day after the fire — the 18th. The train was full of the *Noronic.* People didn't talk about China at all. Or the pennant race. It would have been ten at night when we pulled into Union Station. Ruby went straight to the shipping offices to get a list of the casualties. It wasn't there. She phoned Montgomery's friends. She wept.

I was surprised at the dimensions of her emotion. I didn't imagine her feeling that much for anyone. Certainly not for Montgomery, who was always going off and leaving her. In my mind I compared him to Robbie, and couldn't help thinking how lucky I was to have had Robbie.

The pier next morning was a dreadful sight, the pile of twisted blackened metal, people standing around shaking their heads. Ruby wasn't the only weeper.

I tried to cry but couldn't. I was too scared. The sight of the big ship on its side was so frightening. You can drown in the bathtub, I know, but the green water of the Toronto harbour looked so ... uncaring, slopping this way and that, against piers and small craft and gulls, indifferent to what it touched, animal or vegetable or the hull of the *Noronic*, full of charred dead. Water doesn't care; all it does is find its level.

I'm back in the present, the lights are on, and the bus is lurching as it rounds a corner. The nurses hold on tight. You don't have to, don't even put out Your arms. Good balance.

There's a doctor leaning over me. He listens to my chest with a cold metal ... stethoscope.

I cough. The cold spot shifts.

Do I know you? I ask.

He puts away the stethoscope.

I'm Rose, I say. I cough again.

I know.

Hello, Harriet, I say. She's on my other side, wiping her eyes.

Hello, Mother.

You were having trouble breathing there, the doctor tells me.

Was I?

Your lungs have fluid in them, the doctor says. And you're a little hot.

How does he know? Yes, I am, I say. My voice sounds strange.

The bus slows down. I hear the hiss of brakes and the nurse and doctor grab on to my bed. The doctor says something to the nurse. It sounds like it's in code. How much, the nurse says. The doctor tells her.

What are you doing now? asks Harriet. The doctor explains

about the fluid in my lungs again. How old is your mother? he asks Harriet. Harriet tells her.

Are you sure? I ask.

Harriet smiles down at me. Yes, dear.

I don't feel that old, I say.

How old do you feel?

I remember the morning of my nineteenth birthday. I woke to dread uncertainty, the future a busy field of consequences. What had happened? What had we done?

My new bedroom was still strange to me. I went to the small window. Throwing open the cotton blinds I saw familiar darkness lightening towards day and then — for the first time in months — the sun itself, its rays outflung like a mother's arms, engulfing the whole landscape. My room faced north and a bit east, across the square, and this day was the first day of the year when the sun rose in sight of my window. I stared down at the suddenly hopeful street below, the plodding carthorse and whistling milkman.

I made my bed, took a clean uniform from the drying line across the back of the room. I would have been almost finished buttoning myself when I noticed the small wrapped package on my — well, I guess it was a dressing table, though I never dressed at it. It was a plain deal table with a crate under it for a drawer. I would have written letters there, I suppose, if there was anyone I wanted to write to. I wrote to Mama my first week, and Gert, but they didn't write back. I kept some old bits of cloth in the crate, and a magazine from a florist shop, and a postcard of Victoria Hall at Christmas. I think I meant to tack some pictures to the wall, but I wouldn't have got around to it yet.

I held the flat package in my hand, thinking back. Jack gave me a beautiful pebble from the lakeshore, with our initials scratched on it, and the year: 1923. I'd treasured that for the longest time. Uncle Brian had sent dolls until he lost his job and came to live with us. Mama gave me an atlas on my eleventh birthday, and blushed prettily when I thanked her. A few months later Daddy took it to prop up the end of the bed, said he was sick and tired of sleeping on a slant. I never got it back.

Silver paper, with a true-love bow. The note was sealed in an envelope with a wax seal. I had never opened a sealed envelope before. My fingers trembled as I pulled up the flap.

The notepaper was as plain white and as thick as card. It was unsigned.

GREETINGS, ROSE, ON YOUR BIRTHDAY.

I found that I was holding my breath. I let it out, unwrapped the package, lifted off the top, and beheld the birthday gift, nestled in a bed of tissue. Blue silk, smooth to the touch and light as thistledown. A scarf, pale blue border with white birds figured on a deep blue ground. I draped it around my neck. Oh, my. On my only hanger I kept a walking dress, wine coloured, cut down two summers ago from one of Mrs. McAllister's. I held the scarf against it. I longed to try them on together, but the nearest mirror was in the bathroom and I didn't have time. I replaced the scarf in its box, hid the box and card under my pillow, and hurried downstairs to breakfast. The feeling of dread stayed with me all that day.

Mother, she says, stroking my hand. Mother, come back.

I cough, and cough. It hurts. There's a bayonet in my chest. I can see it, sticking out of me, looking like that film we saw where we worked during the war. A training film for marines, lift and thrust and twist and pull. One and two and three and four, with the lights flickering and the announcer telling us that our boys were learning to stick it to Jerry. We applauded every lunge, every earnest scream, every time the stuffing fell out of the dummies and the boys stepped back with their weapons high. And now I am a dummy and there is a bayonet in my guts. I cough and stuffing falls out of me. But the bayonet stays in, attached to a tube. I feel hot.

Mother, says Harriet, stroking my arm.

I reach up and pat her hand. She smiles. Not her usual scary one. This is a rare and unforgettable smile. Last time I saw that smile was in a dream.

You are alive, I whisper.

She doesn't say anything. The nurse checks my bayonet.

I thought you were dead, I say.

In my dream, Harriet was lying on the pebble beach, with tangled hair and staring eyes. I cried and cried and carried her home, her dead weight in my arms nothing to the weight on my heart. I put her on the bed, and lost myself in darkness, weeping. I tried to pray but the words came hard, passing out of me like stones. I asked You to make my life bearable, to make me understand that the world without my child was still the world. And then on the beach in Toronto, with the smokestacks in the background, I felt my heart lifted, and I thanked You for bringing me back, for making life without Harriet bearable.

I am not here to help you bear things, Rose, You said. Remember? You can bear things on your own. Now, look around you, You said.

And I was back in Cobourg, on the pebble beach where Harriet had drowned, and I turned around, and there was Harriet, alive and running towards me, running with her hair streaming behind her like a banner and a smile like glory on her face. I was so happy, and so surprised — I mean I knew You could do anything in real life, but this was a dream! Pretty spectacular, I still think. When I woke up I went into Harriet's room to check on her and of course she was gone. She would have been thirty by then, left home to live on her own ages back.

You can do anything, and I can't even remember what year it is.

I don't know if the Bluestone case worked out well. I suppose that's a matter of opinion; it worked out fine for Stephen Bluestone, not so well for Harriet. Not that she complained, of course. Harriet never complains. She smiles and bears it, whatever it is: needles, bullies, flagrant injustice, an aging and incompetent mother. She takes a deep breath and turns the page with a heart for any fate. How does that poem go? The teacher used to mark time with a stick on his desk while we chanted: Still achieving, still pursuing, learn to labour and to wait. I remember rain beating on the window.

Harriet phoned to tell me about the outcome of the Bluestone case. I hadn't lived in my apartment for very long, and I was still getting used to the clouds being so close to me.

Hello, Mother, she said.

Hello, dear. You sound funny. Are you all right?

I'm a little tired. They gave the judgment on the Bluestone case this afternoon, she said.

And?

And we lost.

Oh, I am sorry. I know how hard you worked on it, dear.

Oh, that's okay. Stephen is happy, she said.

Something in her voice. Excitement, and fatigue. Outside my living-room window was a big grey cloud, hanging like a kid's mobile, close enough to see every bumpy detail but out of reach even if I stood on tiptoe.

The Appeal Board turned us down, she said. They claimed that the evidence wasn't compelling. The premier made a speech about the importance of the ombudsman's office. And the ombudsman made a speech about the importance of the independent investigative process, giving cases like Stephen's a chance to be dealt with impartially. Sanctimonious old fart, she said.

I was surprised at her. I'd never liked Mr. Sherman, not even when he was a lawyer, but I'd always thought Harriet had.

And then what happened? I said.

I don't quite know, she said. It'll be on the six o'clock news. Why don't you watch it and tell me what you think.

But the something was still in her voice. Are you all right? I asked. I'm tired, she said. I think I'll go to bed now.

Poor Ruby. Poor rum-swilling Ruby, bereft of love, of hope, of will, of friends. Who'd have thought Monty Belinski meant so much to her? She changed after his death. Not on the surface, but underneath she changed, like that house down on Wheeler Avenue when the owner knocked out a wall to make room for his grand piano. This would have been about the same time, back in the late forties. Harriet and I were living two streets over in the same kind of house, with almost the same view of Kew Gardens and the lake. The absent wall turned out to be an important one. Without it the house started to sag. It looked almost the same from the outside, but not quite. A month later it was condemned. And that's how it was with Ruby. She drank a lot, and went out with men, but she always had. She looked and sounded about the same, but inside she was a different person. As if Montgomery had in some way been one of her load-bearing walls.

Probably not an exact parallel, because what happened to the *Noronic* was a tragedy, and what happened to the guy on Wheeler was just dumb. The neighbours felt bad, do You recall, and tried to set up a fund for him so he could afford to rebuild his house. And raised thirty or forty dollars, a week's salary back then. He took it and disappeared, whatever his name was. I never heard what happened to the piano.

The local TV news was read by a young man with an intense voice and puffed hair. It still is, I think. A different young man. Surprising developments in the Bluestone case, he said. Shots of the premier and the head of the Workmen's Compensation Board.

Shots of the ombudsman and Stephen Bluestone, whom I recognized from newspaper pictures. I didn't think he was very attractive. Wide faced and flabby, and his hair too long. All a matter of taste, I suppose. He looked out of place amid the dark panelling, dark suits, bright lights.

I saw Harriet, behind the ombudsman, sitting off to the side. I couldn't help noticing that she had a pimple on her forehead. She always used to get them when she was nervous. The TV camera stayed on her. The newsman was talking with a golden-haired parliamentary correspondent who said she had never seen anything like it. Like a miracle, she said.

The news showed a few seconds of the premier's speech. I don't know what he said because I was staring at Harriet in her dark suit. So professional, apart from the pimple. Stephen sat on the other side of the stage. He looked sad and awkward and in pain, sitting down in a plastic chair with his crutches around his ears and the camera in his face.

There were news stories coming up about sick babies and the dollar and a giraffe at the zoo who wasn't feeling well. Unless it was the dollar that wasn't doing well, and the giraffe that had babies. I thought we would move on, but the camera stayed on Stephen Bluestone.

Watch, now, said the correspondent. The camera kept rolling after the speeches. I saw Harriet beckoning to Stephen from across the room. She looked excited — I tell You I can't see what she saw in him.

Anyway, the camera was rolling and Stephen stood up straight, and walked towards Harriet. Without the crutches. So crippled he can't move his legs without pain, hasn't walked a step in eighteen months, the ombudsman's office and half the local medical association convinced he's a victim, and suddenly, like magic, he walked right across the stage and the crutches clattered to the floor. And everyone's mouth opened wide.

I feel everything at once. I am old and young and drowning, living again a life I never got over. Dying in the present and the past. I'm drowning. I can feel the water bubbling up all around. I want to cry out, but the words won't come. I cough and cough. There there, says Harriet, stroking my hand. Hers is very moist and trembly. I call out but I'm drowning, I'm drowning. The world is moving around me, back and forth, up and down.

You must prepare for the worst, says a voice I know. A nurse's voice. I can see, very fuzzily, a white uniform. My eyes aren't what they would have been.

Help me to sit her up, says the nurse.

I cry out. And again.

I can't tell you how often I've heard that, says the nurse. No matter what they've done in their lives, how old they are, how accomplished, how many children and grandchildren they have, at the end they cry out for their mothers.

Poor dear, says Harriet, stroking my hand.

I'm so hot.

It was a couple of years after the *Noronic* disaster — not too much after, I still had those nightmares, though they were becoming less frequent — that he died. Mr. Rolyoke died, I mean. It didn't make much of a stir in the news. I found out when my bank manager told me that the fifty dollars a month wouldn't be coming any more. I couldn't tell exactly how I felt. I felt like there was a hole someplace. Not just in my allowance, but in my heart, maybe, because I would think of Mr. Rolyoke every month when I got the fifty dollars — and I didn't know why. He'd never visited, not through all of Robbie's and my life together, all of Harriet's life. I didn't cry but I felt as if something long-standing and important had left me. A part of my past was gone forever now. Harriet was grown-up — talking about going on to law school now that she'd graduated. One of her teachers put the idea in her head. A hard worker, Harriet, everyone said so.

You could get a job right now, I told her. Sitting at the table in our room behind the flower shop, smell of mignonette and meadow-sweet and rose. Sun slanting through the north window to light the northeast corner of the room it only hits in the evenings in June; turning it all gold and glowing. You've got your degree, I said. You're a smart girl, anyone would be glad to hire you.

She got that look that said there was no use arguing, and went back to the pamphlet from the Upper Canada Law Society. I went to tidy away the dinner dishes and tried to figure out where the money was going to come from. Not from Lady Margaret, I knew.

Then Geoff asked me to marry him. On his knee, in front of the fireplace in our front room. His face was red with exertion as he climbed back to his feet, puffing. I told him I was flattered, and that he'd have to give me time. Then I stared hard at myself in the mirror and wondered what to do.

You see, I explained to Ruby, if I marry Geoff, Harriet can go to law school. I can't send her on my own.

Geoff owned three bakeries by then, rode around in a big black Cadillac. His nails, that day in the front room, were manicured. I thought I was going to die when I noticed. Maybe he had them done specially, the day he asked me to marry him.

What about you? asked Ruby. Do you love him?

Do I ... He's a nice man, I said. Meaning it like a compliment, but Ruby laughed.

So you don't love him. Well, you've known him forever. Have you taken him to bed?

Ruby!

What? I said something? Pardon me, Miss Joan of Arc, I seem to remember a weekend in New York with one of the Wright brothers ...

I probably blushed. Is that all you can think about? Sex? I said.

Would I have said sex? Right out like that? Really. Well, if You say so.

What do you know about love? I asked Ruby.

She turned away, and I felt bad. Harriet was out with a girl-friend. We were alone, Ruby and I. She was sitting in an over-stuffed wing chair with a drink in her hand. I'm sorry, I said. Have something. Have a ... a mint candy. They were in a bowl on the side table, where everyone keeps their candies. I think they'd been there since about 1937. It's a mystery about mint candies. I don't eat them, so the bowl was always full. I've been to other houses with mint candies, and they don't eat them either, and the bowls are full there too. What a world.

Stephen's face, filling the screen. Questions from all around him.

It was her, said Stephen. The investigator from the ombuds-man's office.

The camera swung around. The ombudsman was frowning.

So you were pretending all along, said the news people to Stephen.

Of course not, he said.

Were you trying to make the ombudsman's office look bad? asked the news people.

Of course not, said Stephen. I tell you, she cured me.

Who?

Stephen pointed. She did it, he said to the news people. It was her.

And there it was on the TV screen, as big as life, my daughter's face, flushed and smiling, and on her forehead a pimple the size of a shiny red dime.

It was a nine days wonder, the compensation case that didn't get any compensation and got better anyway. They couldn't decide if it was a miracle or not. Neither could Harriet. I don't know what

I did, she told me. I wasn't trying to do anything. I remember wishing he would get better.

A nine days wonder, like I said. And on the tenth day Harriet was fired.

Uneaten candies in a bowl. It's a silly idea. Flowers are nicer. More work, mind you, nipping away the dead blooms and refreshing the water — but much more satisfying to look at. There were flowers instead of mint candies in the big house. Plenty of places to put them. The downstairs receiving rooms alone — there were two, a classical and a modern — looked like furniture showrooms, big and busy and crammed full of smooth flat surfaces. And they all needed dusting, the mantels and stands and occasional tables and, in the classical room, a little Louis three-legged thing I was always afraid to touch in case it fell over. Twenty-two rooms in the place, not counting the kitchens and servants' quarters. Twenty-three with the gallery overlooking the front hall. Twenty-three vases for me to polish and fill every morning, twenty-three vases to empty every evening. Plus the two in the cars. Ten bedrooms, two libraries, games room, front hall downstairs (large vase engraved with Ainslie coat of arms, and always at least one spray of purple) and gallery upstairs (small vase with Rolyoke coat of arms), two receiving rooms, small dining room, large dining room, three drawing rooms, and, last but not least, Lady Margaret's upstairs sitting room with the view of the back lawn and lake — I mean river. This was the place in Philadelphia. The house in Cobourg was smaller, the lake was nearer, and there wasn't a conservatory.

What a room that was! Big enough for a ballroom, full of sinuous colourful shapes, growing in defiance of the outdoors. A thick glass door connected the conservatory to the south side of the house. I can still remember the smell of the place, rich and moist and earthy. And warm enough to grow spring flowers in winter. The power of the seasons at my fingertips. Robbie showed me how to change the temperature with a switch on the wall. Not Robbie, Mr. Rolyoke. I walked up and down the rows of plants, feeling like Eve on the sixth day.

I remember kneeling with my back to the door, cutting blossoms for the day. Electric light flickering overhead. Clouds of condensation on the windows.

I sensed his presence before he spoke. I didn't dare turn around.

Beautiful Rose, he said.

I couldn't help smiling. He was always paying me compliments, silly boy. Not a rose, sir, I said. It's a wild orchid.

You flatter me. But I wouldn't have known that at the time. I still didn't turn around.

Bewitching Rose, he said. Humorous, perplexing Rose. When will I be able to see more of you?

I'm sure I don't know, sir, I said. With a delicate hand to my mouth, stifling a yawn. Miriam Hopkins had done just the same thing the week before. Perhaps you'll see more of me when I stand up, I said.

I don't know what I expected: a laugh, a hand on my shoulder. I tensed, but it wouldn't have been with fear. I really don't think it was fear, do You? He didn't do anything, and when I finally did turn around he was gone.

I went back to cutting.

I cannot see. Hazy hazy, the world has wrapped itself in a ... What has the world wrapped itself in, Harriet? I ask, staring up into her battery-operated ... fuck, what are they called? Eyes. Unfuck. Sorry. I don't usually use words like that — You know that. Ruby will have told You. So will Mama.

She's upset, Harriet says to the nurse. What is it, Mother? She bends down and shouts it in my ear. I wince.

I want to sit up, I say.

There there, Mother.

She hasn't heard me. She's holding my hand like it's a TV remote. Point and click. I struggle against gravity, trying to sit up. I pull against her hand, working my long slow course up a hill. I can't make it. I give up and lie back.

Up, I say. Please, up.

Harriet bends down. Tears in her eyes. There I got it that time. Eyes. She lifts me very carefully into a sitting position, holding me in her arms so I won't fall. My daughter. Never had any children of her own, but she has a nice soft touch. There you go, she says.

I nod my head. Let out my breath. About fucking time, I say.

And of course everyone hears that. Harriet stiffens with shock but the nurse laughs. I don't know why I'm so coarse all of a sudden.

The view is breathtaking; I'm not. I cough and try to breathe again, light breaths, my lungs moving slowly and carefully. I look out the window and see traffic lights. I see the shadow of our bus against a storefront nearby. Convenience. Candy, magazines, cigarettes. Two boys are arguing out front. One of them grabs something out of the hands of the other one. The first one grabs it back. It's a magazine. It rips. We lurch on.

After a couple of minutes I get tired and Harriet lets me down onto the pillows. I pat her hand. She nods, blinks. A nurse changes a bag that's coming out of my lungs. The bus sways gently; we must be moving around a bend.

Have you put out the flowers?

Yes, Miss Parker.

All of them? All twenty-two vases?

Twenty-three, Miss Parker. Yes.

Saucy. Here, then — help Jane finish cleaning the breakfast pots and pans.

Yes, Miss Parker.

Demure, eyes down. Just three of us in the back kitchen, and Jane was happy to have the help. A minute later Robbie came in. I hoped he wouldn't say anything about seeing me earlier that morning. Parker would be sure to draw all sorts of conclusions. He'd hardly opened his mouth to speak when I felt the strangest thrill running up and down my spine.

Any more tea? he asked, in a husky whisper. He looked awful, I noticed. Dressing gown and hair all awry.

Certainly, Mr. Robbie, said Parker with a tight smile.

And could I have some honey to put in it?

Of course, sir. That's a nasty throat you have, sir.

He coughed again. Kept me awake all night, he said. I just got out of bed.

Jane splashed hot water on me. I jumped back. Sorry, she whispered.

I didn't answer. It hadn't been Robbie in the conservatory.

Oh, Robbie. I tried to be true to your memory. I don't mean about Wilbur; that was a surprise, and it was about me, not you. I couldn't marry Geoff. Rich, kind, manicured Geoff. I woke up after a bad night — not a drowning nightmare, but a tossed and troubled sleep — and knew what I couldn't do.

I'm sorry, Harriet, I said.

That's okay, Mother.

What'll you do if you can't be a lawyer? I said.

I can still be a lawyer, she said.

Stubborn girl. She'd found out that you could start out as a law clerk, and then write the examinations anyway. She'd even found a lawyer who would sponsor her. What could I say? What would any parent have said? Good for you, I told her. Now eat your breakfast.

The sound at the door was fainter than breath on a window. I knew it more than I heard it. Come in, I said, my own whispered voice ringing like a great bell in the silence. I strained my eyes in the pitch dark of the third-floor back, wanting to see his face, his hand on the door, wanting to see the door opening. But I saw nothing, heard nothing, knew nothing until I felt him next to me.

Happy birthday, Rose, he said.

I didn't say anything.

Beautiful Rose. Do not be afraid, he said. His breath smelled like smoke.

I could not, cannot now, say what happened. Did he speak again? I wonder. I have neither sound nor picture in my mind, only a glorious series of sensations, a kind of sense-movie.

Did he say goodbye? I don't know.

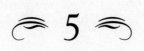

Assumption

Mama, oh Mama, where are you going? Mama, why aren't you there? Will I be safe with you gone? Will you miss me? Will I be safe? Will I be safe?

She didn't say anything. Her eyes were closed. Her skin was whiter than I remembered. I went back to my seat. Harriet was chatting with the young woman next to her, a friendly, animated conversation with lots of nods and smiles. The young woman wore a deep red garment which went very well with her dark skin. One of the nieces. Neither of them paid me any attention. Oh yes, I heard Harriet say. He is nice looking, isn't he?

The woman kneeling behind me whispered over the back of the pew.

You're Rose, aren't you? Mrs. Scanlon's daughter?

I said I was.

You spent a lot of time up there, she whispered to me.

I found a smile for her, a cousin from a small seacoast village, blocky, smelling of cigarette smoke and fish, dressed in purple lilac.

It's difficult to say goodbye, isn't it? she wheezed.

I agreed.

It is that. When my Donald died, I cried for days. I couldn't believe he was gone. I just couldn't believe it. I used to wander around the house like a lost soul, calling his name. I'd put out food and everything. I couldn't bring myself to visit his grave. And then — she swallowed recollectively — about a week afterwards, I saw a mouse. The first one since I brought Donald home from the SPCA shelter when he was just a kitten — and I just broke down and sobbed.

The minister read the burial service like a commercial for soap, cramming a lot of words and feeling into the allotted time. When it was over we buried Mama in a seaside cemetery full of dead Scanlons. The Atlantic Ocean snored and clashed and gnawed away at the rocks beneath us. No one cried, not even Bill. Not even me.

One of Bill's brothers met Harriet and me at the Halifax train station and drove us straight to his house, insisting we stay with him. First time I'd seen any of the Scanlons since Harriet was born. Are you the one they call The Gord? I said.

He shook his head. Red is staying with The Gord, he said. There'll be more room for you here with me and Jessie and the girls. Sometimes they call me Flat Top, he said.

Harriet ran upstairs after one of the daughters to change. I asked after the third brother.

Dog Face was killed in the war. He was in a minesweeper.

I said I was sorry.

That's all right. It's almost ten years, said Flat Top.

You don't mind that your mother will be buried here? his wife Jessie interrupted. She was a soft-spoken kitchen body in a good black dress covered in cigarette ash. The daughters all smoked too, and the youngest wouldn't have been more than twelve.

No, I don't mind, I said.

We've picked a nice spot, she said. There's a good view. Your mama liked to look at the ocean, when she and Bill used to come and visit.

My husband Robbie died during the war too, I said.

But he's not your husband, said the doctor in a hurry, the little one with the head like a soccer ball. He stopped pacing up and down at the foot of my bed to look at me.

He most certainly is, I said. We were married in a church in Philadelphia. Mama was there, and Mr. Rolyoke gave me away. I've only been unfaithful to his memory once, I said. Or perhaps twice.

Mother!

Harriet's mouth was big and round enough to stuff an apple in it. We kept trying to grow apples on the farm, but we only ever had the one crop. Gert's new dad gave us a seedling tree, one year. McIntosh apples, I think, but the blossoms were few, and when the fruit came it was hard to tell just what kind of apple they were — they looked like cherries and tasted like dust.

Maybe only once, I said.

I want that man put away, said Harriet. Firmly. A bit of colour in her cheeks, made her look attractive. He's ... attacking my mother, she said.

Attacking? Are you talking about Robbie? I asked. Robbie would never attack me.

She doesn't think it's an attack, said the pregnant lady, who looked at me for a change. Do you, Mrs. Rolyoke? she said.

From Robbie? I said. Oh no. Robbie is the soul of honour, I said.

The nurse frowned.

Harriet groaned. Mother, she said patiently, tears of frustration in her eyes, Mother, we're talking about Albert Morgan. Do you remember him? In a wheelchair?

Poor Harriet, she thinks I'm a child. Of course I remember Al, I said. He's sweet on me.

I meant it as a joke, trying to lighten the mood. But no one laughed.

Mr. Morgan thinks you're his wife, said Harriet. He calls you Mavis.

Yes, that's right, I said.

She knows it! cried the doctor. Another doctor said something about consent.

The pregnant lady shook her head, her lips pursed up to be kissed. Do you understand, Mrs. Rolyoke? she asked. Do you understand the situation?

I explained. Albert's wife's name is Mavis — used to be Mavis. She's dead, I told them all, nodding my head. Didn't *they* understand what was going on?

And Albert is coming to your room at night — is that right, Mrs. Rolyoke?

No, of course not, I said. He's going to Mavis' room, I said.

The grey weathered wood was hot against my back. I could feel it through my light summer frock. An old cut-down dress of hers with buttons, still billowy in the front, but Mama would have insisted on calling it a frock. Jack took a deep breath as we pulled apart.

Wow! You kiss better than all the other girls, he said.

Why, Jack, you are as fresh as a daisy! I said. But I wouldn't have been upset at the comparison. I was happy to be with him.

Let's do it again, he said, leaning forward, taking my face in his hands, and pressing his lips on mine. I scrunched them up into a kissable bow, like Clara, and let him press me against the side of the barn. The afternoon sun was in my eyes, so I closed them. I smelled clover in front of me, and the barnyard behind, and wood smoke and boy sweat on Jack's clothes.

Let's lie down, he said.

What — on the ground?

No one'll see us. They're all in the east section today.

But I did not want to get my frock dirty.

He leaned close again, and whispered. I seen my mom and dad once, he said.

Mm hmm? I said.

And they were lying down, he said.

They were?

Yup, they sure were. Please, Rose. Please, just this once.

His eyes were so blue, and his hair so curly and dark. His smile was charming and insincere. I liked him a lot.

It's too muddy, I said. And it's getting late. Mama will be wondering where I am.

Please, Rose.

I smiled down at him. One kiss, then — but that's all. No lying down.

We kissed again, and this time he put his hand on me. He reached up and touched me through the thin summer dress. I tried to pull away, but I was up against the barn and I couldn't.

Well, maybe I wouldn't have tried that hard.

He kept his hand there. I imagined my heart beating against it. I felt myself growing under his hand, a blossom unfolding towards the sun. When we pulled away again we were both breathing hard. I know what to do now, he said. I seen my mom and dad.

I've got to go home now, I said.

Didn't you like that? You're all red in the face, he said.

I stared out over the field. Burnham Street wound away in the distance, up the hill. From the top of the hill you could see the spires of St. Andrew's and Trinity United Church in Cobourg. And beyond them the lake, glistening like silver.

Come on, Rose, one more kiss?

No. I turned and started walking across the field.

Tomorrow, he called after me. Tomorrow after school. Same place.

How old would I have been — twelve? And I walked away. Did I?

I suppose I could have asked Ruby to come and stay with me. Two ladies living together, sharing comforts, conversation, fighting over memories and the extra piece of meat at dinner. That made sense. Ruby and I were old friends, and there was room after Harriet left.

She was working for her lawyer downtown; he'd promised to help her with her bar admission exams, and to recommend her to the law society after a couple of years of clerking. I didn't know how she was going to learn law by searching for the titles to buildings and typing up wills, but that was her business, not mine. I was sorry I couldn't send her to law school, but she kept telling me she enjoyed what she did.

I'm helping people, she told me.

That's nice, dear.

And I do good work. Mr. Sherman likes it that I do good work. He tells me so. He appreciates me.

I guess I didn't appreciate her enough. I tried to, but she was so competent, so uncomplaining, so ordinary looking. Hard qualities to appreciate. When she moved out I breathed a sigh of relief. Poor Harriet, I wasn't much of a mother to you.

I didn't move. I liked the neighbourhood. It reminded me of Robbie. I kept the house on Waverley, and the flower shop on Queen. I dusted and paid the bills, looked out the front windows at the streetcars and Kew Gardens and the clock on the firehall. Had nightmares. Tended my garden. Hired incompetent assistants. Bought a television set.

I missed having a friend I could eat with, laugh with, telephone any time of the day or night. I could have asked Ruby to live with me after Harriet left, but I didn't even consider it.

Why are You looking so unsympathetic? I'm a bad friend, as well as a bad mother? Is that what You mean? Should I have invited her to stay? Vomiting in the bathroom every morning, falling down in the hall? Going out and not saying when she'll be back. Going for days without speaking. Staring at me with eyes that aren't seeing me, or anything else. I knew what that was like. I knew exactly what that was like. I didn't want to go through it again.

Stop staring at me so sad and bothered. How do You think I feel? I'm the one who deserted her.

Who are you?

I say that a lot. I'm lying propped against some pillows, staring up into a toasted face and I have no idea who he is. Toast and jam, door jamb, marigold. I don't see the connection. Not toasted — concerned. That's what I meant.

Albert? I say. Is that you?

I'm Sanjay, he says. He takes my hand and holds it gently.

So am I, I say.

Mother, says Harriet, from the other side of me. It would be too much work to turn my head and look at her. Mother, you remember Dr. Berman.

Hello, I say. And cough. He waits until I finish coughing, and wipes my mouth.

It's starting to get dark outside. We're on our way back to the Villa. The danger is over. They've fixed whatever it was that was leaking, and the air is safe again. The ambulance bus rocks a bit as we turn a corner. I'm strapped in, but Dr. Berman has to hang on.

Where's Albert? I ask.

Dr. Berman blinks. Great eyelashes he has, for a man. Long and silky. His dark eyes turn down sleepily at the corners. I don't know, he says.

He went to the other place, says Harriet. Over in East York — I keep forgetting the name, she says.

Not hell — we used to call that The Other Place when we were kids: Be careful or you'll end up in The Other Place! One of the maids at the big house in Philadelphia talked about The Other Place too. We used to tease her about it. Put starch in the cuffs, Abigail, we'd say. If you don't put in enough, Parky will send you to The Other Place. Abigail? Adeline? Some name like that. Her religion was very strict. She didn't last long.

St. Dominic's? says the doctor.

Yes, that's it, says Harriet.

I'm thinking about Albert. He was circumcised. I wonder how that popped into my head.

Mother! says Harriet. She sounds shocked. Oh dear. The thought must have popped out of my head through my mouth. Loose lips sink ships.

The doctor isn't shocked. He gazes very kindly down at me.

Where's Dr. Sylvester? I ask.

He's lying down at the other end of the bus, Dr. Berman explains. He hurt himself when we turned a corner a while back.

Poor Dr. Sylvester, I can picture him lying there all pale and interesting, with lots of attentive nurses. I wonder why this doctor is smiling.

Will we be home soon? I ask.

Yes, he says, standing up, rocking a little with the motion of the bus. Very soon.

❦ ❦

Slips didn't use to happen so often. I was good at keeping secrets. I never told my friends about Uncle Brian killing Daddy. Of course they found out anyway, and were appropriately shocked and excited. Gert shivered, and her eyes went to the shotgun on the wall over the fireplace at her parents' house. Was it a gun like that? she asked. I didn't say anything. Was it? How awful! Did your uncle go Bang, Bang, right in the head? She shivered again, and I overheard her talking to someone at school that week about bad blood in my family. Mind you, this might have been because Billy Burnham had invited me to the pictures. Gert liked Billy.

I didn't tell Dr. Sylvester. No insanity in our family, I told him. No violence. Nothing to cause concern. I smiled at Harriet. I didn't want to spoil her chances with the doctor.

They took their time together, poring over brochures and pamphlets. Every now and then Harriet would look over her shoulder at me, and I'd smile. The doctor's hand was lying on the desk near hers. When he moved it to point something out, their baby fingers brushed against each other.

Downhill, the doctor said. She's going to go downhill. I'm sorry, he said.

Harriet turned to look at me. I smiled encouragingly.

There are waiting lists, the doctor said. It might be six months before she could get in.

And meanwhile? said Harriet.

Meanwhile she'll be losing things, and forgetting to turn off the stove, said the doctor, and inviting dangerous men up to her apartment. I'm sorry, Miss Rolyoke — I know it's difficult, he said, getting to his feet in one smooth sincere motion, the kind of guy who always pulls up the knees of his pants when he sits down, so that there will still be a crease when he stands up again.

They were talking about Joe. I remember Harriet mentioning Your name on the phone when I told her that I'd invited a man who mugged me up for a cup of tea. He didn't really mug me, I told her, because he was so sick and tired he could hardly lift his gun.

Jesus Christ, Mother!

I did it out of guilt. I looked at Joe and saw Ruby, with her hand out. And I took him in and looked after him, not because he deserved it but because Ruby had deserved it.

And he didn't attack me, or rob me. He thanked me for his tea and went away, and I felt better. Looked better too, in my good scarf. The doctor was wrong: I wasn't losing things. But I sometimes hid them and then forgot where. The blue scarf with the doves on it had been in the teapot.

It was still raining when we left the doctor's office. Harriet was quiet on the drive home. She pushed the gear lever back and forth. The engine made noises like an animal in a cage.

My apartment building loomed over the rest of the block. Harriet walked me to the elevator. Do you want to come up? I asked.

She nodded, still without speaking, and we got in the elevator together. Mrs. Collins had her little dog on a leash. Hello, Artie, I said. Then blushed. I mean, Alfie, I said.

Alfie is the dog. Artie is Mrs. Collins' dead husband.

She frowned. Alfie panted. I reached down to pat his head, and he jumped up. Excited little guy. I stumbled, and might have fallen, but Harriet was there to catch me.

Oops, I said. She didn't say anything.

Clumsy of me. Thanks, dear, I said. She still didn't say anything.

Goodbye, Alfie, I said. He yipped.

Harriet had a hold of my elbow as we walked down the hall to my apartment. I shook her arm free to get out my key. I trembled. My hands took longer than usual to find the lock. I wanted to cry out: Can't a body forget? Can't I forget a dog's name and not have to worry? Can't I trip like anyone else? I've got arthritis for heaven's sake. I'm allowed to trip. I'm not crazy. I'm older than I used to be — and so are you. I'm still able. I can still rhyme off the seven times table; I know that liverwort signifies confidence and lobelia dislike. I can recite my Third Form Test Poem. So I close my eyes with the element on, so what? Who am I hurting? The place is cold in the winter anyway. I can use the extra heat.

I don't want you to worry about me, I told Harriet. She nodded.

I'm fine, I said, putting the kettle on the stove to boil and setting out the tea things.

Haven't you ever forgotten a name? I asked her. Or an address or — I stopped. Couldn't think of anything else. She nodded.

Lives of great men all remind us we can make our lives sublime, and, departing, leave behind us footprints in the sands of time, I said. When you were born you weighed seven pounds seven ounces, I said. You were twenty-three inches long. Your father named you after his grandmother. I never knew her. I wanted to call you Gert after my best friend when I was a little girl.

Harriet started to cry.

I poured tea into two cups. Set out milk but not sugar because neither of us takes it in tea. Here, I said. Drink up.

I took a sip. It was the right colour, but it tasted awful. The rain beat against the window. Harriet kept crying. I took a coy look into the pot, wondering what in the name of goodness I'd hidden there this time.

Crying into her drink. What did that remind me of? I'd say 1957, though I could be mistaken. Nothing particularly exciting happened in 1957. Not to me — I'm sure You'd say different. It was a Friday night, I remember, and I'd been out with someone from a seed catalogue company. I got back late for me, which wasn't that late, and found Harriet in my living room, drinking and crying. Come to think of it, she wasn't crying, she was just drinking. Ruby was crying and drinking.

Hello, there, I said.

Oh, Mother, how are you?

Harriet never cried. A couple of scrapes when she was small, and that was it. At Robbie's funeral she'd stood patiently beside me while the graveyard emptied. No, she hadn't — she'd cried and held onto the lieutenant's hand. I'd been the one standing patiently.

Maybe I wanted to remember it differently.

Make yourselves at home, I said.

I hadn't seen Ruby in months. She looked awful, hair plastered down, eyes large, collar open to show a raddled and unwashed neck.

How are you doing, dear? I said to Harriet. I went over to kiss her on the cheek. She smiled. I wasn't used to seeing her drink. It didn't make me feel good.

I had liquor in the house, but I hardly ever touched it. Did I? Well, Harriet didn't. I can't tell You how I felt, seeing my daughter and my — I suppose she was still my best friend, even though I didn't see much of her any more — my best friend tipping the bottle for each other, a pretty pair of tavern cronies.

You should feel sorry for your daughter, said Ruby, speaking very distinctly so as not to slur the words. I asked why.

Because she's never going to get what she wants, said Ruby.

Is that so, Harriet? I asked, and Harriet gave me that scary smile of hers.

That's right, Mother.

Don't worry, sweetheart. There are plenty of men out there, I said.

Ruby laughed, harshly. Like glass breaking.

That's my lie, she said. My line, I mean. She laughed some more. Tell me that one. Tell Harriet some other lie.

I knew better than to try to take the bottle away. I sat down with the two of them in the kitchen. What is it? I said to Harriet. What happened?

I never failed any examinations. Not one. Harriet failed a lot, for such a hard-working girl. I passed all my grades in school. She failed her driver's test too, the first time she took it: The instructor said she was concentrating too hard. I never learned to drive — not even a horse and cart. Billy Burnham gave me the reins, and I slapped the mare's back with them, but you can't call that driving. The mare knew where she was going anyway.

Harriet wrote brilliant essays, but her examination work was always poor. The teachers encouraged her to keep taking the tests, and after a few tries she always succeeded. She even matriculated in mathematics. When she failed the law examinations she sat right down to studying so she could write them again. But then it was too late. They changed the law, so that you couldn't be a lawyer without going to law school first. Harriet would have been — what did I say, 1957? — she would have been twenty-seven. Doesn't seem old, does it? But it was too old to go to school.

So Harriet would never be a lawyer.

She let herself into my apartment, dragging a big suitcase after her. I couldn't remember giving her a key. We'd just said goodbye — Harriet still tearful — a few hours ago. I couldn't remember inviting her back.

Isn't that nice, I said. But what about your job?

I'm taking a couple of weeks off, she said. Harriet was a law clerk with a big firm now. Lots of lawyers telling her what to do. She didn't seem to mind. I'll stay here with you until we can straighten out where you'll be living, she said.

Do I have to move? I said. I don't want to move. I'm comfortable here, staring out the window at clouds, I said.

Mother, you're eighty-six years old. I can't look after you. I can't afford to hire a nurse.

Maybe I'll die before there's a room for me, I said.

Harriet sighed. And then I fell and broke my ankle. No, that's not it. What happened is I broke my ankle, and fell. They took X-rays and went Tsk tsk. Sorry, I told them.

I moved into Warden Grace Villa when I got out of the hospital. Cane and all.

I'm surrounded by fog, drifting through the present like an aban-
doned ship, the wreck of the Rose Rolyoke. Chilling thought. I'm
propped up in my bed in the bus, staring through the window at
familiar trees and parking spaces. Through the fog I can see the
concerned expression on Harriet's face. I can hear the conversation
around me. I can feel my chest rising and falling, feel my
diaphragm working convulsively to force fluid from my lungs. I
can feel my heart beating.

I am tired.

They are carrying bodies off the bus. First off is Mike's mom
with her face covered. I know her, knew her I should say, though I
suppose I am getting to the point where I can know her again. Too
bad I never liked her. Next off the bus is Dr. Sylvester on a stretcher. My head is killing me, he says. Poor man, not so handsome in
his bandage. The orderly drops one end of the stretcher. Dr.
Sylvester swears. Next off is the card player with the hearing aid.

You like him, don't You? I can tell. You reach out and pat him
with Your poor hand. Why? He's a sad and sorry dog, isn't he? He

whines and weeps and forgets what suit is trump. He bosses the nurses and insults the rest of us. No one likes him, not even the volunteers in the gift shop. His card partners make fun of him when he's not looking at them, or when his hearing aid isn't working. So why are You so fond of him? I know You like all of us: Dr. Sylvester, the dead woman, me. It's Your job, after all. But I do wonder why Your face lights up so for Mr. Nathan — there, I remembered his name. Maybe I'll get better after all.

I see and hear and feel through a fog, a curtain of fatigue which makes everything shadowy. I don't mind. I cough. I don't mind. Harriet is bending over me. Her face is close. I can see the pores in her skin. I go inside the pores, inside my daughter, feel her skin sweating, her heart beating. Feel her sorrow. I don't mind. She sighs, and I come out of her and back into me.

You're shadowy too. That's odd, You were so clear a minute ago. A time ago. Am I drifting away from You? I don't mind. I ought to, I know, but I don't.

I am tired.

Harriet is so worried. I try to tell her not to worry. I try to tell her that it is all right, that everything will be all right. I try to comfort my daughter. I cannot make the words come. Something comes but I don't know what it is. I don't mind.

Mother? Mother?

That's Harriet.

Can you hear me, Mother? Mother, do you know me?

Yes, dear. Yes, my darling. I know you. I love you. Don't worry about me. I'm fine. I don't mind.

Doctor! Doctor Berman! Come quick!

I stare up into the doctor's intent face. Luxuriant growth of hair all over: eyebrows, eyelashes, side whiskers. I look past his face, and see the peeling paint on the top of the ambulance bus. And the sign: in case of emergency. When else do you use this vehicle? Oh well, this isn't an emergency. An emergency is unexpected.

I'm cold.

Harriet would never be a lawyer.

And Ruby would never be a wife and mother.

And I would never be a —

My teeth are chattering. I can't understand it. Mama, Mama, help me. What is this feeling? My life, flashing before my eyes?

"Last chance, ma'am." A dignified voice, like Daddy's. A white uniform, like a doctor's.

"She's sinking fast now," says the white uniform.

Overhead, the birds flutter against the bars of their cage. No emergency exit for them.

Almost ninety years; lots to look back on. But there are still questions. My life is passing before me in pain and shadow, and there's so much I don't understand. Maybe You could — would You mind? — answer some niggling questions. For clarification and peace of mind. I'll try not to ask about anything that isn't my business. It's my life, though. I'm entitled to know about me, aren't I?

First off, I guess I want to make sure. Tonight, quietly in my sleep? I guess that's the way most people want to go. Except for those idiots who want a blaze of glory or a beautiful body next to theirs. Quietly, in her sleep. That's what the obituary will say. Am I right? At Warden Grace Villa, from complications arising from pneumonia — or maybe they won't bother with that part. When you're almost ninety it doesn't really matter. Flowers in lieu of donations. Zinnia: *I mourn your absence.* That'd be nice. Or persimmon blossoms: *bury me amid nature's beauty, for I shall surprise you by and by.*

The last time I saw Ruby was in front of Maple Leaf Gardens in Toronto. A weekend afternoon in the sixties. A rally, is that right? Black and white together, we shall overcome. Proud of themselves for doing the right thing. Sounds silly, doesn't it, but it wasn't silly. Now, why would I have been there? Not to march. I wouldn't have cared, would I?

Oh. Are You sure? I would? And my sign said the same thing?

I don't know what to think. I'm pleased. It's not like me to care about people I don't know. I suppose Harriet must have told me. She'd have cared all right. Still does. People from places I can't credit: Bosnia, cardboard boxes, the Philistines ... She cared about everyone but herself, like, well, like You. Yes, I am pleased that I'd have been there.

And marching down Yonge Street to City Hall — that would be the new City Hall, wouldn't it? — I saw Ruby. She was sitting at a counter in a small restaurant, watching the demonstration go by and drinking. Hair in a kerchief, which I'd never have seen her wear before. She was alone, and for a moment our eyes met through the pane of glass and the crowd of singing people. And I thought, I used to know this woman well. Not a day went by but she'd be in the shop, talking about a new hat design she was trying out. Or a new boyfriend. Or she'd be full of a magazine story on the secrets of the ancient Egyptians or how to tell what your perfect mate looked like. I knew her better than anyone in my life then, except my own daughter.

I raised my hand to sketch a little wave, and Ruby looked over my head. And the crowd passed by and me with it. And I wondered — I wonder — did she see me?

I could have crossed the sidewalk, dropped my sign, and gone into the restaurant and talked to her; but Harriet was with me and we were in the middle of ... No, that's not it. I kept marching, and singing about Michael rowing the boat ashore, because I was afraid. I didn't go into the restaurant because I was afraid of what I'd find. Afraid of what she would have become. I didn't want to know.

Did she die by accident a few years later? Was that her body at the bottom of the unsafe fire escape? The newspaper article gave her name but not her address. I went to the funeral wondering if it could be the same Ruby Wellesley. I never found out because the casket was closed. There were no other mourners. The landlord paid for the funeral.

I wonder if she saw me that afternoon in the crowd of marchers. Did she recognize me? Perhaps she was scared too. And I wish. Oh I wish. I wish I could have the chance again. Poor Ruby. I'd run into the restaurant and take her by both hands, the way she used to greet me. I'd invite her back to the shop to live. I'd give her flowers. Hazel and Star of Bethlehem: *reunion, reconciliation*. And yew: *I am sorry*.

Lady Margaret was not a mother-in-law out of the music halls or TV situation comedy. She did not interfere, did not appear in our lives at all, Robbie's and mine. That morning in Cobourg, in front of the summer place, with Harriet in my arms and the horse waiting behind us, was the last time any of us ever saw her.

Did she know about the regular payments into our bank account, I wonder? She must have, if she stopped them.

Isn't it odd that Mr. Rolyoke died without a will. The lawyer in Philadelphia was so embarrassed. I used to wonder if ... if maybe there was a will, leaving something to Harriet, if not to me. I suppose not. That sort of thing happens in movies.

Lady Margaret lived a long time, didn't she. Even longer than I'm going to. I'm surprised she didn't move back to England after Mr. Rolyoke died, but she preferred to hang around Rittenhouse Square with the dust sheets and the mice and her disappointments.

I wonder how she knew Harriet? You're not going to tell me, are You — not my story. She did know her, though. How else to explain the clippings? Her niece Estelle found them after she died, and phoned me because my number was written across the bottom of the one from the Canadian news magazine. *A Miracle?* was the headline. The story was all about the Bluestone case. There was a photograph of Stephen Bluestone shaking hands with Harriet. Lady Margaret would have got the phone number from the Toronto book, I guess; Harriet's number would have been unlisted.

I still don't understand the reason for the other clipping in the file folder. A Wild West show from the turn of the century, complete with war paint and snake oil and knives thrown at a spinning girl. And in front of a crowd of people, sporting, said Estelle, a pair of sideburns like the prophet Amos in her Bible at home, was Mr. Rolyoke. Uncle Rolyoke she called him. He had his hands on an old woman's forehead. Except for there not being a question mark at the end, the headline was the same as Harriet's. Quite a coincidence.

Funny that Lady Margaret would keep that shot of Mr. Rolyoke; you'd think she'd want to hush up her husband's dubious beginnings.

What? Is it humankind You're smiling at, or just me and my stupidity?

Anyway, Estelle asked did I want the photo, because otherwise she would just throw it out. I said no thanks. I already had a copy of the *A Miracle?* article. I thanked her for her trouble. I didn't really know the Rolyokes very well, I said.

If he had left everything to Harriet it would have made a difference, wouldn't it? She'd have been a lawyer. Don't think I'm complaining; he didn't owe us anything. He'd been more than kind to me and Harriet both. I think well of him — better than well, really. Kind of — don't laugh. Kind of the way I think about You.

You're welcome.

Anyway, a legacy from Mr. Rolyoke would have made a real difference to Harriet. And to me, I suppose.

What was that? Stephen Bluestone? Yes, You're right of course. It would have made a difference to him too. He'd have been a cripple.

All these would-have-beens.

Rise, my love, my fair one, and come away. He used to say that to me, sitting with me in my empty window frame, staring up at the moonlit night. He always spoke so beautifully, David Lawrence Godwin did. I loved him so much; it was an honour to love a man like that. But I'd like to know one thing, I told him. Do you ... love me back? Just a little?

Of course if he'd answered, Yes, a little, then I'd have hated it. And if he'd answered, No, not at all, I'd have ordered him away. But he always gave the correct answer — My love, he'd say, I do not love you a little. How could I love you a little? I love you more than the stars and moon, more than the grains of sand in the beach, more than the leaves on the trees. David was big on enumerating the size of his love, the number of bakery trucks he owned, the volume of dough — cubic tons, I think, I pictured rooms full of the gooey stuff — that his employees turned, every day, into bread and rolls. Did I say David? Geoff. I meant Geoff. Geoff the charitable baker, not David the fictional soldier, wounded in The War.

How could I ever have got them confused? I must be worse than I thought. I'm reminded of the time Harriet and I discussed my memory problem, back before I broke my ankle. We were up in the apartment, drinking tea and staring out at the grey clouds that looked close enough to touch. Would it have been the only time we spoke of it? Maybe. Just because I don't remember any other times doesn't mean there weren't any.

You're going to have to take me to the doctor's, Harriet, I said. I'm starting to forget things.

Like what? she said.

How should I know what? I said. I'm the one forgetting. You should be telling me what, I said. You're the competent one.

She turned away as if she couldn't look at my face. We've already been to the doctor, she said. We were there this morning. You forgot the visit.

I thought back, but couldn't make a picture. Not that one anyway. What did we talk about at the doctor's office? I asked.

Forgetting things, she said.

Good, I said, and she nodded Mm hmm. We drank tea for a moment. It began to rain. Did the doctor cure me? I said.

She snorted. I've always been able to make her laugh. Evidently not, she said.

Geoff was a good man, a hairy man who said he loved me. And not just me. Harriet is such a nice girl, he said. So talented. Do you remember her wind band meeting in my shop, Rose? My first shop, he added. I remembered.

Such a smart girl, he said. Arguing your case in front of the judge — and just a child at the time. When you told me that story, Rose, I was so proud of her. Proud the way a father is proud of his daughter. I was honoured to attend her graduation. And I would be honoured to be a second father to her now.

It was summer, but it must have been late because the front room was dark. We were alone, me at the window, Geoff on one knee in front of the fireplace. I turned on our new floor lamp. Geoff squinted up at me, shading his eyes from the trilight bulb. Say yes, Rose, he begged. Make me the happiest of men.

Oh, Geoff, I said. This is so sudden.

Not for me, Rose. He smiled, stretching his face flat so that two quiffs of nostril hair poked out, like a pair of rabbits peering from neighbouring burrows. When his face relaxed they receded again. It was a phenomenon I'd noticed before.

I'm not poor, he said. The baking business has done well. Do you know how many trucks I have at my beck and call? he asked.

I said I didn't know. Guess, he said.

Why didn't I love him? Why? A good man, hard working and never mean, he'd earned his success. He deserved a chance to show off to the woman he loved. I didn't resent his delivery trucks or his manicure. He wasn't ugly, and anyway I'd have been forty years old — forty-two, if that was the year Harriet graduated. Who was I to pick and choose? It's not as though John Gilbert was hanging around our back door.

It was a bit of a shock seeing him for the first time on screen. *Arabian Love*, wasn't it? He reminded me of my imagined portrait of Lieutenant David Godwin. I gaped all the way through the movie, and made sure I got to see *While Paris Sleeps* and *Truxten King* and *Cameo Kirby* when they came to the Arlington Cinema. It was as if I'd drawn a picture of a flower never before seen, and then found it in a meadow. Anyway, by the time I might have married into the bakery business he was out of pictures, Hollywood's and mine. 1952? Would that be right? I didn't have George Brent hanging around the door either.

Come on, guess how many trucks I have, Geoff demanded. Guess high.

A million? I said.

Yes, smile. I can smile with You now, but it wasn't a nice thing to say. Geoff was a gentleman, he reddened and climbed to his feet. Please think about my offer, he told me, pressing my hand in his. His nails gleamed in the lamplight, diamonds stuck on a hedge of thick dark hair.

I'll never forget your kindness before the war, I said. When you gave away food every day to the poor people who couldn't find work.

Why didn't I want to marry him? Why didn't I say yes and swoon into his arms?

Was I envious of his success? Doesn't seem right. I think — now this is funny; I feel funny right now — I think it was his wanting to be Harriet's second father. I remember shivering when he said that, thinking to myself, *She already has a second father.*

But why? What's scary about a second father? Gert had one. What am I missing? Was I thinking about You? Was that the point? Even thinking about it now I get a shiver.

Maybe it's the cold. Isn't it cold! And noisy. I can hear the rush of water. It's a huge noise, a flood. I'm choking on it. Water in my lungs. Choking to death. Drowning from inside. Old man's friend, they used to call pneumonia. With friends like that ...

᧠᧠

Oh, Mama. Why are you so cold? Don't turn away. Don't you know who this is? It's me, Rose. It's me. Your daughter. Don't be cold. Don't be cold. Oh, Mama! Help. Help me now. I'm cold. I want you. I want you. I'm cold. I want you! I want! I want!

"Poor thing."

Is it You? A dazzling white uniform, a worried expression. A huge and powerful pair of hands.

I feel the last grains of life trickling away, salt through the egg timer. My three minutes are up. Harriet is a shadow. The nurse is a shadow. They are staring down at me. Harriet is holding my hand. Dr. Berman is a shadow. Is it his white uniform?

"Poor thing."

No. It's another white uniform. Brighter, and with gold braid. Is it Yours? Do You pick me up and button me inside Your uniform jacket? I'm still cold.

Noise all around. People screaming, running, sliding past. Water everywhere. Splashing over the floor. Furniture bumping around. Bodies floating.

Goodbye, doctor. Goodbye.

Goodbye, Harriet. I wonder why you never married. None of my business, I suppose, but a mother can't help wondering.

I wonder how many Germans Mr. Davey killed before his tank blew up?

I wonder why Parky is so mean to me? She likes to look at me. I can tell.

I wonder why Gert is mad at me. I never even kissed Billy.

I wonder why the corn doesn't grow. Daddy is disappointed, I think. Only he never says so. He never says anything. Victor, can you understand Daddy? Mama and I can't.

Isn't that a lovely sight: a carpet of flowers spreading over the field in front of me. Let's see, I have daisies, hollyhocks, larkspur, dianthus and petunias.

Goodbye, Harriet. Goodbye. Your hands are so cold.

Look, Uncle Brian's car has Diamond Impermeable tires. Guaranteed to withstand punctures.

I want Mama. Mama.

Old and young and drowning. Is this the future I never had, or the past catching up to me? I feel everything. I feel warm water inside me, cold water all around me. Sea water. I feel Mama's arms, and Harriet's, and Robbie's, and Yours. Phrases drift back to me: a telescoping of time, says Dr. Sylvester, is one of the effects of the disease. Breaking down the barriers of time in the brain, so that she lives in the past as vividly as in the present.

So rich my life would have been, if not for that sea water. Filled with love and striving, fear and hope, and an occasional miracle. So full. And so real.

No one suggests prolonging my life, I see. Are You sure of that? Harriet — such a sensible, competent girl — isn't going to cry, Save my mother at all costs! Another day, even another hour, is worth any kind of ... You're sure? Ah well. I can't blame her.

I want to live.

I'm not cold any more. I'm not anything. I can feel a gentle rocking motion, back and forth, back and forth. The water's cold but

I'm not cold. I can hear voices from a distance, saying, Careful. Put her down gently. I can hear someone crying. Harriet cried at her daddy's funeral. I never cried at my daddy's. Poor Harriet. Poor Daddy.

I want to cry now, but the tears won't come.

I can see You very clearly. You look like that housewife on TV, who never gets her man's attention even though she's cooked his favourite meal. I'm sorry. I love Your pot roast. I don't mean to take You for granted.

Remember the times I prayed — would have prayed — when I was a little girl lying in my bed in the friendless darkness, watching the shadows on my ceiling and walls, cloud against moon, tree against snow, listening for Daddy to fall against things, and Mama to sigh? We had *Give us this day* in school every morning, but I didn't say that. Look after me tomorrow, O Lord, I'd say. Remember? Tomorrow, not today. As if You couldn't look after me at that moment. As if the night — the present — was beyond even Your power to control. And that by asking for future help I could put off the moment of trial and disillusionment when I realized that You couldn't help me at all. That, maybe, You didn't exist. Poor me.

Faith is hard. Even now I can't help feeling that You'll disappear the instant I look away, the instant I close my eyes; that You could disappear whether I close my eyes or not. How do I know You aren't a figment of my own desire? I know how powerful that can be.

I want my life. Is that what You're offering — now?

My life. Can You help me?

I want it. I want it so much. If I had shepherd's purse I'd give it to You. Do I mean shepherd's purse? White-flowered weed, grows in a cornfield — You know it. Yes, shepherd's purse. *I offer you my all.*

You're smiling, but not meanly, to make fun of me. You can't be mean, can You? You're smiling hard but there are tears in Your eyes. I can see them glinting on Your lashes when You blink. Ruby could be wicked: Some of the things she'd come out with were horrible, but so funny I couldn't help laughing. Maybe it was the way she said things: It's all in the timing, she'd tell me. I'm surprised You don't joke more. For someone with Your sense of timing, comedy would be a natural fit.

It is a matter of faith, isn't it? All right, here is my prayer right now. I'm still lying down, staring at blackness. And I'm praying. I, Rose, ninety years in the dying, ask You to look after me — not in the future, because I don't have one; and not in the present, because it's slipping away faster than a drunk's inheritance. Look after me in the past.

That's right. If Your grace is truly infinite, it knows not space, nor can it be confined in time. Look after my youth, will You? Look after me in my cradle. Let Your grace wash my childhood clean. Be most careful of my growth, my young womanhood, my own experience of love and trust. Let Your face be turned towards me as the years run back. Please. Heal my hurts, infuse me with hope, bring me to faith, to love. Bless the girl I was. Keep her in Your care. Watch over me all the days of the life I leave now. Amen.

The noise is deafening. Tugs and pleasure launches of all sizes crowd the water. Flags fly, whistles screech, people cheer. Passengers line the rails of the big liner for their first sight of land in four days. Liberty holds her torch aloft.

It is a beautiful spring morning, sunny and warm, with a fresh breeze that covers the water in little flecks of white, as if God, a mischievous wedding guest, has been throwing rice despite stern clerical injunctions against such unseemly expressions of goodwill.

A young couple, shivering and somewhat frowzy from lack of sleep, stare wide-eyed at the approaching skyline. "I do hope your brother is waiting for us," says my mother.

A steward, heavily laden, jostles us from behind.

"Careful, there!" says my father.

"Sorry, sir." The steward peers over the top of the cases he carries. "Oh, dear. Is he all right?" My mother carries a restless bundle in her arms.

She frowns.

"Cute little fellow." The steward straightens up and totters towards the port side companion way.

"It's a girl," my mother calls after him. "A baby girl."

The wind is picking up. "Mares' tails," says my father, looking at the sky.

"Will it get rough, dear?" It has been the smoothest passage so far. Everyone has commented on it.

"Not in the harbour," says my father.

I squirm in my mother's arms. I want to get down. "There there," she says. My father bends down to stroke my smooth small cheek with his finger.

"Mama," I say. "Mama. Dada. Bud."

Mother smiles. "Bud" is the way I say bird. The family keeps a pair of pet birds in a cage. They are in the cabin now, along with the rest of the luggage.

"Seagull," says my father, pointing. "D'you see, Rosie? Seagull."

"Bud." I'm not looking at the seagull. I wave at a spot in midair, beyond the deck rail. I think it's a bird.

The harbour mouth at last. The tugs — a whole fleet of them — are in position. The vibration of the great engines, for so many hours a constant in our lives, fades away. The noise from the harbour swells like an angry boil. It seems as if the whole city has turned out to watch the big ship come in.

"Papers," calls a deck steward. "Today's newspapers. *Times, World, Globe, Post.*"

"But where did you get today's papers?" asks my mother.

"From the tugboats, ma'am." The steward is a cockney with a pock-marked face and restless eyes. The braid and buttons on his white uniform sparkle in the sunlight. Mother smiles nervously and steps back.

Nearer and nearer. The gulls wheel majestically, spoiling the effect when they open their mouths. The harbour is choked with small boats. The tugboat crews are swearing themselves hoarse and thrusting the most importunate small craft out of the way with their own well-fendered bows.

The great ship blows three blasts on its whistle. As if they'd rehearsed it for weeks, all the other ships in the harbour blow three blasts in reply. The din is enormous. The silence after it is equally remarkable. And in that silence, moving silently as a great ghost herself, the liner glides into its waiting slip.

Acknowledgements

Even though some of my best ideas come to me during housework, books are not created in a vacuum. My agent, Dean Cooke, and editors, Maya Mavjee and Martha Kanya-Forstner, were encouraging, hard-working and attentive to detail. Joe Kertes' unbridled enthusiasm for the project got me going on it. Kim Echlin liked an early draft of the first section so much she arranged for publication in the *Ottawa Citizen*. I would also like to express my appreciation to the Writers' Development Trust, for timely assistance. Finally, I must thank my family — especially Bridget, for crying during the good bits.

About the author

Richard Scrimger's first novel, *Crosstown*, was published in 1996 to widespread critical acclaim and was shortlisted for the 1997 City of Toronto Book Award. One of his children's books, *The Nose from Jupiter*, won a Mr. Christie's Book Award in 1999. His stories about life with his four children have appeared in newspapers and magazines across Canada, and were published in the collection *Still Life with Children*. Richard Scrimger and his family live in Cobourg, Ontario.